Destination Brides

Will the trip of a lifetime lead to the altar?

When Molly, Maya, Jenna and Eve bid on bucket-list-worthy vacations at a charity auction, they each embark on the adventure of a lifetime at glamorous destinations around the world—but will they find love that lasts forever along the way?

Travel with them from the comfort of your armchair in

Summer Romance with the Tycoon by Donna Alward

Available now!

Swept Away by the Venetian Millionaire by Nina Singh

Available in July!

And look out for

Jenna's story by Barbara Wallace in August

Eve's story by Liz Fielding in September

D1357934

Dear Reader,

I love writing "armchair travel" stories. The research is so fun! And while it's not quite the same as being there (my bucket list is very long), it sure is a lot cheaper on the pocketbook.

Don't get me wrong. I'd rather do the actual traveling. But another side to traveling in my books and not in real life is the ability to face some of my fears without actually, you know, having to face them. In *Summer Escape with the Tycoon*, I drew on my own experience with zip-lining as I'm scared of heights, but I did it anyway...and loved it! On the other hand, I also hold Molly's fear of being flipped over in a kayak, and I addressed that without having to actually face it myself. I know—chicken. Maybe someday.

Either way, it all ends up with Molly and Eric facing both physical and emotional fears in this book, and I hope you enjoy their sense of adventure as much as I do!

Best wishes,

Donna

Summer Escape with the Tycoon

Donna Alward

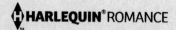

Recycling programs for this product may not exist in your area.

ISBN-13: 978-1-335-49939-4

Summer Escape with the Tycoon

First North American publication 2019

Copyright © 2019 by Donna Alward

Printed in U.S.A.

Donna Alward lives on Canada's east coast with her family, which includes her husband, a couple of kids, a senior dog and two crazy cats. Her heartwarming stories of love, hope and homecoming have been translated into several languages, hit bestseller lists and won awards, but her favorite thing is hearing from readers! When she's not writing she enjoys reading (of course), knitting, gardening, cooking...and she is a *Masterpiece Theatre* addict. You can visit her on the web at donnaalward.com and join her mailing list at donnaalward.com/newsletter.

Books by Donna Alward

Harlequin Romance

Marrying a Millionaire

Best Man for the Wedding Planner
Secret Millionaire for the Surrogate

Cadence Creek Cowboys

The Last Real Cowboy
The Rebel Rancher
Little Cowgirl on His Doorstep
A Cowboy to Come Home To
A Cadence Creek Christmas

Heart to Heart

Hired: The Italian's Bride

Visit the Author Profile page
at Harlequin.com for more titles.

To Barb, Nina, and Liz...but especially Liz, because being in a continuity with you is one of *my* bucket-list items. xx

Praise for Donna Alward

"This is Donna Alward at her best.... Her stories are homey and comfy and gentle—this one is no different."

—*Goodreads* on *A Cowboy to Come Home To*

CHAPTER ONE

THE LAST PLACE Molly Quinn wanted to be tonight was at the Merchant Seafarer Resort, wearing a snug cocktail dress and her feet in a new pair of heels that added a good three inches to her height and blisters on each of her pinky toes.

A parking attendant took her keys and she handed him a generous tip before taking a breath and entering the luxurious lobby. Cool air washed over her and she made a conscious effort to tamp down her irritation. It didn't help that she'd been in heels since seven this morning, in the office early to prepare for a deposition. After a grueling day with clients who'd acted more like children than adults, she'd changed at the office, left an hour early and then fought the traffic to get to the resort on Nantucket on time. Tomorrow she had to be in court by ten, so she had no option other than to drive back to the city tonight and get in at an ungodly hour. Why had she done this again?

She had to admit, it was a gorgeous spot. Positioned above a white-sand beach, with sloping grounds leading to the ocean, the Seafarer was a Nantucket icon: grand, timeless and a bastion of wealth and opulence. But Molly would have much preferred sitting on her balcony, sans footwear, sipping on a glass of rosé to attending such an event, no matter how wonderful the cause.

"Molly! You made it."

Ryan O'Neill appeared out of nowhere, striding across the lobby as if he owned it, dressed in perfectly tailored Armani. Tall, with striking blue eyes and a hint of Irish red in his chestnut hair, he garnered attention wherever he went. Lately he'd received a good amount of attention because of his divorce from a somewhat obscure actress— one who was more recognizable now because of the public nature of the split. Ryan had brought the money into the relationship, and Molly had been the lawyer in charge of ensuring he kept as much of it as possible.

Moreover, she liked him, and they'd become friends of a sort. He was a train wreck at the moment on a personal level, but he was a nice, fun guy, and she hadn't been able to say no when he'd asked her to attend tonight's dinner and auction with him. No one wanted to attend these things alone and make for an odd number at a sponsored table—especially when you were the sponsor.

"Ryan." She smiled genuinely and held out her hands. He took them and gave them a squeeze, then leaned forward and kissed her cheek in greeting.

"Thank you for coming tonight. There's nothing worse than attending these things alone."

She grinned up at him, feeling a little of her annoyance dissipate. "You're welcome. Sorry I'm a little late."

"It's just getting started. Let's get you a glass of wine, shall we?"

"Just one," she cautioned. "I have to drive back to the city tonight."

"Ah, yes. No staying at the hotel tonight, I remember." He put a hand at her back and chuckled a little. "You do like to follow the rules."

"Always." She arched her back and moved away from his hand slightly, not wanting to settle into the touch that was both solicitous and…a little too familiar. She looked up at him, all Irish roguishness and twinkling eyes, and suppressed a sigh of irritation…

and maybe a hint of regret. "Which is why I accepted your invitation tonight when I said no to the others. Officially you're no longer my client, so I'm not breaking any rules."

"Yet."

She raised an eyebrow. "Still not staying the night. But nice try," she teased. If she thought he really meant it, that his overtures were more than flirting, she would have refused the invitation. But she knew he was still a bit too raw from his divorce to do more than be charming.

He laughed now as he guided her from the lobby to the ballroom where the dinner and silent auction for a new opioid treatment center was being held. The other reason she hadn't been able to say no to him was because she knew that it was a personal cause. Ryan's brother had been in and out of rehab since he was twenty-two. Ryan had confessed to her during one of their meetings that finding the painkillers in his wife's bag had been a critical moment in deciding if he wanted their marriage to continue. He'd immediately had Molly's sympathy. And if she were being honest, the ugliness of his divorce had exhausted her and made her wonder if her exorbitant fees were, in fact, worth it.

But that was behind them now. The ballroom was stunning. Tables were bedecked with ivory and gold linens, and flower arrangements, heavy with lilies, sent out a pungent, exotic scent. The room was already half full of other guests, who mingled with longstemmed or highball glasses in their hands. Chandeliers dripping with crystal winked over the assembled crowd, and soft music played. A waiter approached and Molly took a glass of something white and cool as Ryan asked for a whiskey.

It was a good cause. There was food. She had a good-looking, fun date. And she still really wanted to be home and out of the shoes and dress and Spanx that kept her figure smooth and a size smaller beneath her dress. As the Lycra dug into her ribs, she heard her mother's voice in her head, reminding her of the extra ten pounds she always carried, and how certain dresses simply weren't flattering. One day she was going to burn every single slimming garment she owned and say the heck with it.

For a while she and Ryan mingled, then moved on to peruse the auction items.

Each one represented a grand adventure, a trip of a lifetime. Displays were arranged with some featuring promotional videos, while others had representatives in attendance. She gawped at the offerings. There was an African safari. A castle in Provence, among the heady scent of lavender fields. Italy—including gondola rides in Venice, a wine *agriturismo* in Tuscany and a side trip to Malta and the famed Blue Grotto. The rain forest in Costa Rica and mountain climbing in Nepal. Bids had already been made on some of the adventures, and she sipped her wine and wondered what it would be like to actually take a trip like that. These were bucket-list items, she realized. Bucket lists to help those, like Ryan's brother, who may never have the chance to do any of their bucket-list items if they didn't kick their addictions.

It made her pause and think about her complaints that were really, in the overall scheme of things, small stuff. She had all this money and a great career and she wasn't happy. So maybe it was time for a change. For some time she'd felt that family law was a mistake, and a bit too soul-destroying. The trouble was, she wasn't at all sure what *would* make her happy.

Ryan was chatting to someone a few feet away and Molly stopped at a table, her attention caught by a monitor where killer whales curved through the waves, their dorsal fins straight and tall. The shot shifted to a group of kayakers sliding through the water, with huge sequoia trees, rolling hills of grape-vines and a view of the ocean from a luxury hotel room. The words *Island Outdoor Adventures* crossed the screen, with the smaller words *Vancouver Island, Canada.*

Canada. Maybe not the most exotic location in the world, but she'd occasionally traveled to Montreal or Toronto for conferences and she'd loved the country. She stepped closer to the table and picked up the glossy brochure. The adventure promised a variety of experiences, most outdoor, with luxury accommodations to pamper even the most particular guest.

"Find something you like?"

Ryan's voice sounded by her ear and she half turned. "Maybe?"

He picked up a brochure and flipped it open. "Kayaking with killer whales? Zip-lining in the rain forest?" His teasing eyes swept over her. "That doesn't sound much like you, Molly."

A sliver of indignation seared through her. How would Ryan O'Neill know what did or didn't sound like her? Sure, they got along well. He'd been a good client and they'd had some fun conversations. But he didn't know her. Not really.

Unless he did. Unless she really was as boring as his tone made her sound. Her whole life she'd followed a set plan, hadn't she? Never a misstep. Of course, it meant she hadn't made many mistakes. But she'd never taken any risks, either. Regret didn't just happen because of what a person had done; it could come from what they hadn't done, too.

"What does sound like me?" she asked carefully.

He shrugged and took a drink of his whiskey. "I don't know. Work. You work a lot and when you're not working you're doing things that are associated with work."

"Like tonight?" she asked, a bit sharply, and noticed the teasing look in his eyes dimmed.

"I didn't ask you here as my lawyer. I asked you as a friend."

"I know." She sighed. "I'm sorry I'm so snippy." It really wasn't him she was annoyed with. He'd struck a nerve. She did work too much and didn't cut loose often. Huh. Scratch often. Try never.

Nope. Molly Quinn did exactly what was expected of her, right on time and by the rules. After her brother's death at a young age, it had fallen to Molly to wave the family banner, and she'd done it with pride. Valedictorian of her high-school class. Full scholarship for her undergrad and a degree at Harvard Law—naturally—to make her parents proud. And then, also as expected, she'd joined the family firm. She was now a full partner at the ripe old age of twenty-nine, in Quinn, Colton and Quinn, the premier family-law practice on the East Coast, outside of New York. The Colton was honorary now, as her father's partner had retired two years ago. At nearly thirty, she'd dissolved dozens of marriages without ever having been married herself.

She'd been close, once. She hadn't been willing to become anyone's accessory. She'd worked too hard. She'd wanted…more.

So Molly lived a very nice life. A very nice, insular, boring, sheltered life doing exactly what was expected on the appropriate time line.

"Are you thinking of bidding?"

She shook her head. "No, I don't think so." She hesitated. "Maybe."

"Well, you could always start the bid on this one and then it might prompt someone else to step up and get the ball rolling.

The higher the bid, the better for the rehab center."

He made a good point, so she looked at the itinerary again and bid a bit lower than the trip's worth. What the heck.

Thirty minutes later, they sat down to dinner. Ryan was a prominent vascular surgeon, and the table was filled with several of his colleagues and their spouses or dates. Molly smiled and spoke at the appropriate times, but much of the conversation eluded her and her mind kept darting back to the Vancouver Island adventure. What would it be like to do such a crazy thing? She'd never been particularly athletic, and she'd certainly never left on a whim to do something so impulsive. But just because she never had didn't mean she couldn't.

Dinner was delicious, the seafood fresh and the vegetables locally sourced. The music was lovely, conversation was witty and sophisticated, and Molly was bored out of her mind. With her mother's caution still ringing in her head, she refused dessert, some sort of terrine that looked divine and probably contained a zillion calories. When plates were cleared she was mad at herself. Why shouldn't she have dessert if she wanted? Why did she always have to deprive herself? It certainly didn't make her a better person.

That was it, she realized. Following the rules, following the path that had been laid out before her, hadn't made her a good person. The truth was, she didn't really know who she was, other than a good lawyer. She felt sad about that for a few moments, and then she set her jaw.

The only person who could change that was her. And maybe it would take getting away and going out of her comfort zone to really discover who Molly Quinn was and what she wanted.

She excused herself and went back to the silent-auction offerings again. At the Island Outdoor Adventures table, she hesitated and looked at the bidding sheet. Two other bids were there, and disappointment rushed through her.

Screw it, she said to herself and reached for a pen. She hastily scribbled a new bid. She wanted this now. Wanted to run away and have her own personal-revelation moment. Just because she'd never done those things didn't mean she couldn't; that was why they were bucket-list items. And just because they'd never been on *her* personal bucket list didn't mean they weren't once-in-a-lifetime experiences. Maybe she wouldn't *Eat, Pray, Love* her way to enlightenment, but a change of scenery and a challenge might be exactly what she needed to gain some personal clarity.

As the evening progressed, she made her way back to the table again and again and upped the bid. At one point she wondered if it was going too far and cringed at how much of a hit her savings account would take if she won. Then her competitive streak would pop up again and she'd write down her next bid.

The evening's emcee announced the final ten minutes of bidding. A man who looked to be in his midthirties stepped up and raised an eyebrow as he read her latest entry, then picked up a pen and scribbled something down. Not to be outdone, she went right behind him and raised the bid by two thousand. Her heart pounded as she returned to Ryan's side. The bids were now sitting at twice what the entire trip was worth.

She checked her watch.

Mystery man met her gaze and quirked his eyebrow again. He was handsome, she acknowledged, with thick dark hair and chocolaty eyes that warmed as a hint of a smile tipped his lips, a challenge if she ever saw one. She gave a nonchalant smile and a shrug, as if to say, "Whatever." There were six minutes left.

He walked over to the table. A smile played over his lips as he saw her entry. And then he upped the bid again.

He stepped back, smiled broadly and walked off.

She was dying to know what he'd written down, but she was already in too deep to make any rash moves or give him the opportunity to outbid her again. She shrugged, then turned to Ryan and made small talk with their host, Kit Merchant, as the seconds ticked down in her head. Kit had arrived late and was regaling them with sailing stories. Molly listened with half an ear, the other part of her brain busy ticking away the moments until she could make her move.

When there were just thirty seconds left by her count, she sauntered over to the table, wrote her name, looked at his bid, took a deep breath and wrote a new number only one hundred dollars greater than his final bid. She put down the pen and turned around. He was about to step forward when the emcee called, "Bidding is now over. No more bids will be accepted."

She'd won.

CHAPTER TWO

ERIC CHAMBAULT TOOK a deep breath and stepped out of the elevator, a heavy sigh escaping his lips. He'd had an acquisitions meeting early this morning. Then he'd headed for the airport in order to make his flight. Montreal to Victoria was a long trip, and he'd enjoyed the few hours with his phone in airplane mode. Once he'd landed, though, it had buzzed and rung nonstop. On the last call, he'd told his assistant that every call for the next ten days was to be directed to the appropriate VP and that he would be out of contact. Then he did something he hadn't done in nearly eight years. He turned it off and left it off.

He'd be lucky if his blood pressure wasn't skyrocketing again. Thirty-four years old and his doctor had cautioned him about stress and told him to take a vacation. He wasn't interested in lying on a beach somewhere. Instead he'd taken the advice of one of his friends and started looking into outdoor adventures. Joe had gone on one a year or so ago in South America and said it had been the best trip he'd ever taken.

Initially, Eric had thought it would be a vacation for two. Then the divorce papers were served and it was clear no couples trip would be on the agenda. What followed had been eight months of legal wrangling that had cost him an exorbitant amount in billable hours. In the end, he'd paid his legal bills and hers, too, as well as a settlement that still made him grit his teeth: just over thirty million in a lump sum. The only saving grace was that he wouldn't have to worry about paying alimony every month for the next four or five decades. Murielle had got her money and he was left with a bad taste in his mouth and a heart full of disillusionment.

He waved his key card over the hotel-room door and it turned green. With a twist of the handle the door swung open and he stepped inside, pulling his large suitcase behind him. He could have had a bellboy bring his things up to the room, but right now he didn't want to see any other people. He wanted to be alone. Take a shower. Perhaps have a nap before the group dinner tonight, which he was dreading. Because people.

But maybe a shower and a power snooze would put him in a better frame of mind. He just wasn't there yet.

A sound touched his ears and he frowned. Water running? He looked around and spied a Vuitton case on the luggage rack. What the hell? Was there someone in his room? Eyebrows knit together, he strode toward the bathroom and opened the door.

The string of profanity that greeted him, complete with splashing, had him shutting the door immediately. But not before he'd had a chance to spy long, soapy legs, the tops of some very lovely breasts that were covered with bubbles, and a flashing pair of blue eyes below dark hair, damp from the steam in the room.

A man could notice a lot in two seconds, apparently.

He spoke through the now closed door. "Um…you're in my room."

There was a splash and then her words came, sharp as knives. "You're in *my* room and I'll thank you to get out. Now."

Eric sighed and pressed his fingers to the spot at the top of his nose, where suddenly all his tension had centered. "I just checked in, and I assure you, this is my room. But I'll wait for you to get dressed. I'm sure the hotel will get this straightened out and you'll be in your own room in no time."

And probably a smaller one. At least he'd been put in an executive room, complete with a lavish king bed, a comfortable seating area and a view of Victoria Harbor that was incredible.

There was a great deal of splashing now and the sound of water draining. Eric stepped back from the door and took a breath, then went to the window to look outside. Seriously. He just wanted to relax for an hour. Was that too much to ask? This was supposed to be a first-class hotel with top-notch service. How did this sort of mix-up even happen?

Noises sounded from the bathroom. Unhappy noises. Apparently a little peace was indeed too much to ask for.

When the door opened he schooled his features and turned around.

And nearly swallowed his tongue.

She was angry; there was no doubt about that. Her blue eyes, framed by sooty lashes and set above lips that remained full and plump even as they were puckered in displeasure, snapped at him. She was wrapped in a hotel robe, and it was big on her, but he still had the picture of her legs in his head and the front of the robe gaped just enough to offer a tantalizing glimpse of cleavage.

He swallowed. Hard.

"I suggest you take your bag and go right back down to the desk," she snapped.

He offered what he hoped was a calm, pleasant smile. "I think we should go down there together. I'll wait for you to get dressed."

"I don't think so."

"But possession is nine-tenths of the law," he reminded her. "So I'm not leaving. That—" he pointed to the bed "—is my bed and I'm going to be taking a nap on it, so let's not be difficult."

A smile touched her lips. "Don't quote law at me," she said, a bit of mockery in her tone. "I'm a lawyer."

Ugh. "Of course you are," he muttered. He frowned as he looked at her face more closely. There was something unsettlingly familiar about it, but he couldn't quite place it.

"What's that supposed to mean?" She put her hands on her hips, which only made the gap in the front of the robe wider. He tried really hard not to stare, but damn, she was attractive. There was no denying that. Where had he seen her before?

"It just means that the only thing worse than having someone mistakenly in my room is having a lawyer mistakenly in my room." He knew it was an unfair thing to say, but seriously. The whole reason he was on this trip alone was because of his divorce and he was still bitter about how much he'd lost in the settlement.

"Wow. All right." She moved to the desk and picked up the phone. A few moments later she hung up and turned to face him. "If you'll excuse me, I'm going to get dressed. Someone will be here in a minute to sort this out. Please let them in."

She grabbed something out of a closet, slammed a few dresser drawers and disappeared into the bathroom again.

He gawped at the bathroom door. Holy cats, but she had cool dismissal down to an art form, and she knew how to sling orders, too. If he weren't so annoyed, he rather thought he could use someone like her in his company. The way she'd sashayed into the bathroom hadn't escaped his notice. A memory tugged at the corner of his mind, but before he could try to grab it, she came back out at the exact same time as someone knocked at the door. They both moved to answer it, but Eric sent her a quelling look and stepped forward.

"Good afternoon, Ms. Quinn, Mr. Chambault. I'm Paul, the assistant manager, and I'm so sorry for the mix-up." He tried a smile. "Mr. Chambault, I'm afraid there was an error upon check-in that resulted in you being given the keys to Ms. Quinn's room."

The look on her face was triumphant.

Eric hesitated a moment, searching for the right words rather than the ones spinning through his head. "Accidents happen. If I could be shown to my actual room, that would be great."

Paul's smile turned into something that resembled a grimace. "Unfortunately, your room isn't quite ready yet. It'll be about an hour. We're happy to keep your bags for you in the meantime, and you're welcome to wait in our executive lounge and enjoy some refreshment. I promise that you'll be in your room and settled before your group dinner this evening."

"Group dinner?" Ms. Quinn—that was what he'd said her name was—stepped into the conversation. "You're not with the adventure tour, too, are you?"

Oh, Lord. He didn't want to go through

the next ten days with her in the group. Suddenly that solitary sitting-on-a-beach thing was looking very enticing—why had he chosen this over the tropical vacation he'd initially planned? He met her eyes and was surprised to see something that resembled embarrassment in their depths, not to mention her flushed cheeks. Whether caused by embarrassment or from the heat of the bath, he didn't know, but the trip was ten days long and he didn't want this inauspicious event to set the tone.

"I am," he replied and nodded. "I guess there's nothing to be done about it."

There was an awkward pause. Paul began taking Eric's suitcase and carry-on bag to a bell cart while Eric and Ms. Quinn stood awkwardly in what was, apparently, her room.

"Sorry for the inconvenience," she offered, slightly more subdued than she'd been earlier. He was about to snap back with a sharp retort when he put himself in her shoes. She'd been relaxing in a bath when a strange man had walked into the room. Of course she'd been angry…and she had every right to be. Even if the mistake had been in his favor, he could understand her reaction.

"And I'm sorry for freaking you out," he replied. "It's been a long day."

Her lips twitched a little, and those pouty lips curved up in a smile. Then a smile with teeth...and then a light laugh came out of her mouth.

He chuckled a little, too. "Not exactly a great icebreaker, was it?"

"No," she answered and stopped laughing. Her face was more relaxed now, though, and something shimmered in the room between them. Maybe it was just the awareness that he'd caught her in a fairly intimate situation. Whatever it was, he was uncomfortable with it.

"I'm Molly," she said, stepping forward and holding out her hand. "Molly from Massachusetts."

"Eric," he answered, taking her hand. It was still warm from the heat of the water, and soft. But her grip was firm and he liked that. The memory slid back. Damn if she wasn't the actual reason he was on this particular trip. "Wait. You're—"

"We're all set here, Mr. Chambault." Paul reappeared at the door, interrupting Eric's sentence. Eric dropped her hand, still a little shaken by his sudden realization. He'd seen that smile before. That soft, plump mouth with a teasing grin. It had been the mention of Massachusetts, though, that had really tipped him off. She was the woman from the hotel. The one who'd outbid him. He'd wanted the trip badly enough that he'd booked one for himself anyway. He'd never dreamed they'd be on the exact same one.

"I'll see you at dinner," he said, then stepped away. Maybe she wouldn't remember him, and he'd just pretend they were complete strangers. Because really, they were.

Ten days. She'd be a part of his tour group for the next ten days. One thing he knew for sure: he couldn't ever interrupt her bath again. The last thing in the world he needed was a holiday romance. And Molly from Massachusetts could be very tempting, indeed.

Molly let out a breath as she stepped into the private dining room. She could do this. Good heavens, a room full of strangers was not an unusual thing, and they were all on holiday. No one was worried about division of assets or custody agreements. So why was she so nervous?

She wiped her hands on her linen trousers and admitted to herself that it was all due to Eric...whose last name was something French. She only remembered that because the assistant manager had called him Mr. Something or Other. But it fit. His voice was low and smooth, with just a hint of an accent on certain words. Together with his thick dark hair and chocolaty brown eyes, it was no wonder her sexy-ometer had gone a bit haywire the moment they'd shaken hands.

But that wasn't all. She'd tried to have a short nap herself, and it had been in that moment just before nodding off that she'd remembered those eyes. She was good at placing people and he was the one who'd lost the bid on this very trip at the benefit this past spring. The big question was, did he remember her?

She was the last to arrive in the dining room, and there was one vacant seat at the table. And, of course, it was directly to the right of Eric. Her nerves went crazy again, sending butterflies winging through her stomach. Oh, well. Might as well get used to it and set the tone. After all, they were going to be in the same group for the next week and a half. At least he didn't seem to remember her. She could just pretend that she'd never laid eyes on him before. No problem.

She went to the table and pulled out the chair. "Wow," she said easily. "I didn't expect you to save me a seat."

He turned his gaze to her and she felt the little jolt of electricity again. "I didn't," he said dryly. "Five minutes ago you would have had a better selection."

"I'll survive." She sat down and reached for her napkin. "Has everyone ordered?"

"No. Just our drink orders."

A server came by and Molly ordered a pomegranate martini, and by the time it had arrived, food orders were being taken. She decided to start with a beet salad, then a main of duck. She listened as Eric ordered his dinner. Then she took a sip of her cocktail.

He'd seen her in the bath. Ever since, she'd wondered exactly how much he'd seen. She hoped her breasts had been covered. She'd definitely had her toes up on the faucet, but had the other bubbles provided cover for… everything else? Her face heated and she put down her glass and reached for her water.

"Something wrong?" he asked, reaching for a slice of bread. He smeared honeyed butter on the top and took a bite.

"Of course not." She faked a smile and straightened. "Did you have your nap?"

He nodded. "I did. I didn't have the distraction of a wonderful view."

Discomfort slid through her. "I'm sorry?"

"My room is considerably smaller than yours, that's all."

She reached for the martini again—this could be a long evening. "It's probably because I got a deluxe package." She chanced a glance in his direction. "It's really just a bucket-list kind of thing."

He buttered another corner of his bread. "So what about this trip is on your bucket list?"

"Oh, well. Uh… Nothing? I mean, I don't really have a bucket list." Too late, she realized she'd contradicted herself, something she never did in her profession. Why was she so flustered?

Their salads were served and she picked up her fork. But Eric hesitated and she paused with her fork stuck in a piece of endive.

"What's the matter?"

He shrugged. "I guess I'm just confused. If this is a bucket-list trip, but you don't have a bucket list…"

Right. And the last thing she wanted to do was get into her motives and personal life. Instead she smiled. "Oh, that. Well, I'm a bit of a workaholic. I hadn't really considered an actual bucket list, but I decided that I could do with some time off and something exciting. Trip of a lifetime, amazing experience, yada, yada."

He nodded and the mood relaxed. "I get the workaholic thing. You're a lawyer?"

"Yes, family law. Partner in the family firm. Dissolving marriages since 1982, when my dad started his own practice with a friend."

"Oh."

That was all he said, and the air seemed to cool around them. To her surprise, he then turned away and began talking to his neighbor on his left.

Maybe her first impression had been right after all. Rude and entitled. Maybe there'd been a moment of something that had flashed between them, but his snub just now had been real. Fine. She ate her salad and struck up a conversation with her neighbors, a husband and wife from northern Alberta who were involved in an oil-and-gas company. Their previous expedition had been walking the Camino de Santiago in Spain, and soon they had her laughing at some of their stories.

The duck was succulent and tasty; a glass of wine after the martini helped take the edge off her irritation with the man on her left. By the time dessert arrived, she was more than ready to head to bed and get a good night's rest before tomorrow's beginning of their trip.

She'd ordered the hotel's signature cake, rich with hazelnut and cream, and promised herself she'd only take three bites and have a strong coffee. Eric had momentarily turned back, and when he saw the dark liquid in her cup, he gave it a side eye. Was it possible she'd been mistaken? The man beside her now didn't hold any of the warmth and humor that she'd sensed in the mystery bidder back on Nantucket.

And why did she feel like tonight she'd been judged and had come up lacking in some way? Even her coffee got a sideways glance.

"It won't keep me awake, if that's what you're thinking," she said.

"I didn't say anything."

"You didn't have to. Listen, I don't know what I did or said to put you off, but maybe we should just agree we got off to a rough beginning and then stay out of each other's way during the trip."

"It's your job."

"Pardon?" She put down her fork.

He faced her. "It's not you. I mean, this afternoon was embarrassing, and yes, I'm judging you on something superficial, but I just went through a major divorce. Let's just say it was nasty and I lost a lot of money."

"And you lost your wife, too, right?"

He gave her a cold look. "Don't act like you care about that. Her lawyer certainly didn't. It was all about the numbers, and putting a price tag on the six years we were married. Apparently I was such a horrible husband that she deserved five million a year in compensation."

She knew that wasn't how it worked, but that he was speaking from a place of bitterness. Moreover, he had to be loaded. Thirty million? He'd paid his ex-wife thirty million dollars?

"Your lawyer should have done better for you," she said firmly, picking up her coffee cup. "Children?"

"None, thank God." She sloshed some of her coffee and he shrugged. "Not that I dislike children. Quite the contrary. I'm just glad we didn't have any to get caught up in a custody battle."

She relaxed a little and met his gaze. "I know."

"Do you?"

His tone was accusatory but this time she let it bounce off her. She did know. Her parents had stayed together but custody agreements were tough, and if anything made her cry in her job, that was it. Children were not possessions or assets. And sometimes there was an internal struggle between fighting for her clients' interests and trying to do what was right for the kids.

"I think I'll go up now." She put down her cup and started to push out her chair.

"Nantucket," he said, his voice firm and definitive. "You outbid me, Ms. Quinn."

Her cheeks flamed as she put her napkin on the table. "Yes—yes, I did. I wasn't sure you remembered. Mr....?"

"Chambault. And I remembered." His gaze was hard, his body language sharp and edgy as he reached for his drink. "You held out to the last minute."

"I play to win."

"Not everything is a game."

"No, but strategy matters. Good night, Mr. Chambault."

She turned on her heel and walked away, her heart pounding. The evening hadn't gone as she might have liked, but at least she'd ended it with the last word.

CHAPTER THREE

MOLLY STRETCHED IN front of her window and took a deep breath, taking in the view. Dawn had come about an hour earlier, and now the morning sun sparkled off Victoria's inner harbor and the pristine white sailboats docked within it. She'd slept soundly; despite the turmoil of dinner, the mattress had been most comfortable, the pillows plump, and the dose of melatonin she'd taken for the time-zone changes had carried her off to sleep. Today they'd leave for the Cowichan Valley, where they'd visit several wineries, do some tasting and spend the night in luxury before heading for their more "rustic" adventures.

She was just about to head for the shower when her phone rang. A quick look at the screen showed it was her father, and she let out a sigh before answering. He'd thought her trip was foolish and ill-timed, but then she realized that her parents had kept to the same schedule for most of Molly's life. A condo in Antigua every January for a week. Two weeks in Europe in May, before it got too hot. They stayed in the same places—the right places—with the right people and never varied. The idea of taking off on a whim had caused such an uproar that she'd had to postpone her originally planned trip and rebook.

Now he couldn't even leave her alone for the ten days she was gone. She didn't want to resent it, but she did. A lot.

"Good morning, Dad," she said into the phone.

"It's noon here."

"I know." She rolled her eyes. "What's up?"

"I wanted to keep you up to date on the Morrison-Cleveland case. She's asking for less alimony in exchange for full custody."

Molly pinched the top of her nose and closed her eyes. "Which arrangement benefits the children more?"

"He's our client, Molly. Not the children."

A familiar feeling of rebellion rose into her throat. "Well, you know how I feel about this. Look, I know he's our client but he had affairs and got caught, and then got stuck with a DUI charge. They're going to have a more stable life with their mother at this point, and it would be great if we could keep them from using their children as leverage. He's not a family guy, Dad. He'll pay less in alimony and you can negotiate a fair visitation schedule."

"I knew that was what you'd say."

"Then why did you call?"

"You dropped the ball on this one. The idea is that he gets to keep his kids and a bigger portion of his money. You know that."

Molly sat on the edge of the bed. "I'm not sure I agree."

"You'd damn well better, for the fee he's paying. Molly, we didn't get where we are by being soft."

There was a long pause, and then Molly said, "I'm on vacation, you know."

"Oh, believe me, I know."

The words *I'm sorry* sat on her lips. For leaving, for leaving her caseload with him, for disappointing him, for whatever else she might need to be sorry for. For being the child who'd survived? But she didn't say it. She was so tired of apologizing when something didn't go exactly to plan. Of daring to actually try to have a life of her own. She couldn't always be Jack. His death hadn't been her fault. But placating her parents was her fault. She'd got into the habit and now had a hard time getting out of it.

"You know you can do this in your sleep, Dad," she replied instead. "You don't need me there."

"Not really the point, Molly. You left your clients in the lurch."

Now she was getting truly irritated. "So you've said. But even you take a vacation. I'm back in ten days. The firm won't fall apart." She sighed and stood once more. "I'm late, so I'm going to have to cut this short. Bye, Dad."

She hung up, knowing she'd catch hell later for hanging up on him. But seriously. Wasn't she entitled to a holiday? And at twenty-nine years old she could figure out when and where she wanted to go. She didn't need his approval, though for some reason both her parents seemed to think she did. She turned off her phone and shoved it into a shoulder bag. Her stomach growled. If she didn't grab some breakfast soon, they'd be on the road and she'd be running on empty.

She called for a bellhop to get her cases, and once they were collected she adjusted the strap on her bag and headed for the coffee shop. What she needed was a huge coffee and something to take away the gnawing in her gut. In a matter of minutes she was sipping on strong, black brew, with a cranberry muffin in her other hand and a banana tucked into her purse.

The group was congregating in the lobby, waiting for their transportation, chatting up a storm. Molly knew she should join in, make some acquaintances. That was what last night had been for—breaking the ice. Right now she held back. She was still irritated by her father's call and that work life had intruded when she'd been gone only twenty-four hours.

Eric was standing by the sliding doors, talking to the couple she'd met at dinner last night. He was relaxed and smiling, and suddenly he laughed at something, the warm sound carrying across the lobby and sending goose bumps over her arms. She lifted her coffee and took a gulp, the hot liquid burning her throat.

He looked over and the smile slid off his face as he offered a basic polite nod.

Well, bully for him. He had a very closed mind, judging her for her job just because he was divorced. It wasn't her fault that negotiations hadn't gone his way.

She wondered why they'd split in the first place. There was always a reason. She'd heard them all in her years in the firm. A few had caused some raised eyebrows but little surprised her now. She looked at him, standing with his weight on one hip, his hand tucked into the pocket of pressed khakis and his shirt taut against a broad chest. Appearances didn't count for a whole lot when it came to a lifetime of happiness, but she couldn't discount the way her breath caught just a little when she looked at him. It wasn't just that he was handsome. There was a quiet confidence that was magnetic. Yesterday he'd been insufferably overbearing when he'd barged into her room, but something told her he wasn't always so abrasive.

So he didn't like what she did for a living. So what? She hadn't come on this trip as some sort of way to meet a man or hook up. She'd done it to expand her own horizons. To take charge of her own life and live a little. Eric Chambault wasn't going to stand in the way of that, so she adjusted her shoulder strap, put a smile on her face and made her way to the congregated group standing just outside in the sun, waiting for the luxury passenger vans that would take them to their next destination.

Eric tipped back his head and let the sun soak into his face. Their tour guide, Shawn, had told them that the first day of the trip was their easiest one—wine tours and tastings. While it wasn't really on the extreme adventure list, the tour centered on showcasing what Vancouver Island had to offer.

Right now Eric was sitting on a patio just outside the town of Duncan, with the sun beating down on his face and the smell of tart wine and freshly cut grass touching his nose. On his next deep breath, he thought he could taste the tang of the ocean in the air. Maybe this was the "easy" day, but the relaxation came as a welcome relief from his hectic schedule.

He was one of the first back from the tour of the cellars, but his solitude was short-lived as the other eleven in the group made their way, talking and laughing, to the stone patio for lunch. He straightened and smiled as people approached, already flushed from stopping at two other wineries before their late meal. A light laugh caught his attention and he looked up to see Molly—Ms. Quinn—smiling up at someone he'd met named Rick, who was a real-estate developer from Arizona. Rick was at least fifty with a booming laugh, so Eric wasn't sure why on earth he'd feel the least bit of jealousy.

Maybe because when Molly looked at Eric

she tended to scowl, rather than smile, like she was doing right now.

The group congregated around the collection of tables, and within moments the staff began delivering wine selections and platters of local cheese, freshly baked breads, olives, roasted vegetables and fruit. Once again, Molly seemed like the odd person out, like him. Everyone else was either part of a couple or traveling in pairs with a buddy. His skin tingled as her skirt brushed his arm when she pulled out a chair and sat beside him.

"This was a consequence I hadn't anticipated," he said quietly as she picked up her napkin.

"What's that?"

"Being a single in a group full of doubles. It seems as if we're paired up once again."

"I apologize."

Her voice was soft but there was an underlying steel that made him smile. "I should be the one apologizing," he replied, feeling a bit like a jerk. "I shouldn't have used the word *consequence*. It has a negative connotation."

And yet the correct word seemed just out of reach.

She met his gaze, and he was momentarily lost in her clear blue eyes. "I'm sure that as we go on, we'll make friends in the group so we're not always stuck with each other."

As in, she was also stuck with him.

A server poured wine into Molly's glass and she tasted it, savored and nodded. He indicated he'd have the same. The pinot blanc was buttery and with notes of pear, and while Eric tended to prefer reds, he found it really quite nice. For a few minutes they focused on filling their small plates with selections from the platters. Then Eric turned to her and offered an apology.

"I'm sorry for what I said last night. I'm still bitter from the divorce. But clearly it isn't your fault."

"Just people like me."

He swallowed tightly, unsure of how to respond. She wasn't wrong.

"Like I said last night, your lawyer should have done better for you," she suggested, spearing an olive on her plate. "I would have."

He wasn't sure how he felt about that. "It wasn't just about the money," he said quietly. "That stings, but I'll make it back. It wasn't my whole fortune. Not even close, really."

He wasn't trying to brag; it was the truth.

She chewed and swallowed thoughtfully.

"Were there significant grounds for the divorce?"

"You mean, did she catch me cheating or something?"

Molly raised an eyebrow and popped a piece of cheese in her mouth.

"No," he answered tightly. "No, I didn't cheat. And I don't think she did, either. We just…didn't suit."

"What are you leaving out?"

Her gaze had never wavered from his face, and he realized it both put him on the spot and had the consequence of making him also feel incredibly heard. For the first time, he admitted where he'd been at fault. "She called me unavailable. As in… I work too much. That she wanted a husband, not voice mail and an empty bed."

"And was she right?"

He took another gulp of wine, the pang in his heart a reminder of how he'd failed. He had loved her. And he'd tried to provide her with a secure life, which in the end she hadn't appreciated. Ironic, considering she was very secure now. "She wasn't exactly wrong about work."

Molly sat back. "So you're taking this vacation to…"

He stared out over the sloping vines and

sighed. "Well, to unplug for the first time in years, really. It was hell not turning on my phone today."

She laughed then, the sound brushing over him like a summer breeze. "Oh, I wish I'd had your willpower. My father called me early this morning about a case. And a chance to twist the knife a bit that I've abandoned the family firm."

Eric's mouth fell open. "By leaving for less than two weeks?"

She rolled her eyes and nodded. "I'm usually the 'yes' girl. I was getting tired of having my whole life planned and scheduled by someone else, so I bid on the trip." She met his gaze again. "I was supposed to do this a month ago. Instead I had to finish up a Very Important Case." She sipped her wine and grabbed a slice of bread. "Just so you know, they're all Very Important Cases."

"My deals, too. I'm in acquisitions."

She considered a moment. "So you, what? Buy, strip and resell?"

"Pretty much."

"You're like that guy in *Pretty Woman*. He didn't build or make anything, either."

"I make money," he suggested and then laughed a little at himself. "That's why I was in Nantucket. I was working on a deal in Boston. Going to the benefit was a bit of goodwill on my part. Not that it wasn't a good cause. And hey. It got me here, and I would have missed walking into the wrong hotel room and being flayed alive by the sharp edge of your tongue." He gave a sideways glance. "You must be terrifying in the courtroom."

She burst out laughing, then sighed. "Oh, I suppose I am. But it's exhausting. It's…a mind-set, really. I have to try really hard to leave work at work. You and I have something in common, you know."

"What's that?" Curious now, he leaned closer to her, and a soft floral scent reached through the other delicious aromas of the day and hit him square in the gut. She smelled so…pretty.

"We both deal with The End." She plucked another olive and chewed it thoughtfully. "You buy up businesses in trouble. I dissolve relationships in trouble. It's not exactly the most optimistic and hopeful occupation in the world. It can be downright depressing."

"So why do it?"

She sat back. "Ah, now that is the question, isn't it?" Her voice was deceptively light, and she was saved from answering when a server came out with another platter, this time with handmade fruit tarts.

They both selected a tart but he wasn't deterred. "So why are you a divorce lawyer if you don't like it?"

"Because I'm twenty-nine years old and a full partner," she said, but her gaze didn't quite meet his. She bit into the tart and crumbs went fluttering to her plate. "Why are you in your line of business?"

He looked out over the vines for a moment before turning back. "Because I joined the company right out of school and worked my way up. And then I bought it when I was thirty."

"And that was…"

"Almost five years ago."

He was thirty-four and what did he have to show for it? A huge bank balance but not much else. No wife, no kids… God, if he didn't have time for a wife, how could he ever be a good father? He wouldn't even know where to start. His own father had taken off when Eric was twelve, leaving him, his brothers and his mom to pay off the debts he'd racked up as well as paying the bills. Eric got a paper route and mowed grass until he was old enough to work. Then he got a job with a landscape company in the summer and did snow removal in the winter to help with finances. By the time he was seventeen, he was running his own crew at the company and it paid his way through university—he'd done his degree at McGill so he could stay at home and commute, saving dorm costs. His brothers had all taken similar paths. Work. Some postsecondary schooling at community college. Except they'd gone into business together, while Eric had moved on.

From the moment his dad had abandoned his responsibilities, Eric and his brothers had begun shouldering them as a team. When he decided not to join in the car dealership with them, it had been seen as a betrayal. His relationship with his family had suffered because of it. And yet if anything happened to the dealership now, Eric knew that he'd be able to step in and provide his family with the security they'd need. He never wanted any of them to go through what those early days had been like. He was the oldest. Perhaps the younger boys didn't remember as well, but he did.

"Where'd you go?" Molly's soft voice interrupted his thoughts. Her tart was gone but his hadn't yet been tasted.

He gave his head a little shake. "Sorry. Just thinking."

"I could see that. But it didn't look like happy memories."

He shrugged and picked up the cherry tart. "Honestly, I was just realizing that I haven't really stopped working since I was twelve years old."

"Then a vacation is long overdue," she answered and lifted her glass. "I know you're not crazy about divorce lawyers, and I'm not crazy about autocratic people who barge into my hotel room. But maybe we can call a truce? Make a pledge of civility?" She lifted her glass. "What do you say? To long-overdue vacations."

A pledge of civility? His problem wasn't going to be being civil. It was going to be reminding himself that he wasn't interested, because she was more intriguing by the minute. He lifted his glass anyway. "To long-overdue vacations."

CHAPTER FOUR

THEY ARRIVED AT their next destination—a lodge just outside Campbell River—late in the afternoon. Her bags were already waiting in her room; one of the company vans had taken the luggage ahead while the passengers whiled away the day at the wineries.

The previous night's accommodations had been posh and luxurious; tonight's were less ostentatious but equal in comfort and services. When Molly was taken to her room, she was treated to an expansive view of the mountains out the large window and a sumptuous king-size bed with a fluffy duvet and plump pillows. The decor was simple and expensive, but there was something inherently calming about it, from the clump of fresh lavender and sweet grass on the pillow to the soothing bath salts at the edge of the oversize soaker tub. According to the brochure, the lodge was often used for yoga and spiritual retreats. As she let out a deep breath, she could understand why. It was perfect.

They were on their own for dinner, so she first headed to the spa for the Ayurvedic massage she'd booked as part of the package. Soft music, scented oil and sure hands meant that an hour later she emerged feeling incredibly relaxed and about ten pounds lighter. The masseuse had encouraged her to drink a bottle of water before leaving the spa, and by the time she returned to her room, she didn't feel like going to the dining room, so she called down and ordered room service.

The fresh pasta with pesto and feta perked her up, though, and around nine o'clock she thought she might head down to the hot tub for a quick dip. She left her dishes outside the room and slid on a pair of flip-flops before heading to the outdoor hot tub.

The air had cooled once the sun had gone down, and Molly discovered half their group lounging in the huge tub. She hung up her robe and left her flip-flops under the hook, and then stepped into the steaming water wearing her modest one-piece swimsuit, hurrying so her body was on display as little as possible. The couple from Alberta were soaking near the steps, and she offered a smile as she sank up to her armpits in the bubbles, letting out a happy sigh.

"It's lovely, isn't it?" asked Joan, the woman beside her. "We had dinner and decided to go for a dip and I'm so glad."

"I had a massage and dinner in my room. But then I thought, why not?" She smiled at the other woman. "I came on this trip to take advantage of what it had to offer, so here I am."

"Speaking of taking advantage of the amenities," Joan said, her voice a little lower, and Molly turned to follow the path of Joan's gaze. Her body heated at the sight of Eric coming across the wood decking in his bare feet.

"Oh. It's not like that," Molly muttered.

"Are you sure? You seem to be together a lot."

"We're the only singletons on the trip. There's really nothing."

Except for the little knot of attraction that settled low in her belly. He wore swim trunks and a T-shirt, which he stripped off and tossed on top of the pristine white towel from his room. She put on a smile and kept her shoulders at the same level as the water, increasingly self-conscious of her figure in a bathing suit.

He got in, gave her a wink and slipped across to the other side of the pool, where he began chatting with other guests.

"See?" She turned to Joan and smiled. "Definitely not pairing up."

Joan laughed then. "Sweetie, I'm forty-eight years old and I don't get fooled easily. You can't take your eyes off him."

Good thing the pool was hot and her cheeks were already flushed. She shrugged and said, "I didn't say he wasn't good-looking. I'm not blind."

Joan laughed again, and then they settled into a conversation, getting to know each other a little better and chatting about the wineries from earlier today.

People started getting out not long after. Molly considered it, but Eric was still here and she was still self-conscious about being in her bathing suit. Thank God she hadn't worn a bikini. She was so confident in some ways, but not about her figure. There was no flattering cut or supportive undergarment to help her now. The little pudge at her belly and flare of her hips would be on full display if she stepped out of the water.

So she waited.

And so did he.

And he met her gaze—his was warm and alluring as a smile crawled up his cheeks.

Nerves went from her belly to her chest, making it hard to breathe. He slid across the hot tub to her side, not too close, and sat on the seat at the edge, his arms spread along the top of the tub on either side. "So," he said, and she noticed that his hair was damp at the edges, making it nearly black.

"So," she parroted, trying to act nonchalant. Huh. This usually wasn't a problem. She had a reputation for being cold in the courtroom. Unflappable. Right now she was definitely feeling...flapped.

"Come here often?" He lifted an eyebrow, and she couldn't help it. She giggled a little.

"We have to stop meeting this way," she replied, playing into the cliché.

"Of all the gin joints..."

She really laughed now and pushed her damp hair out of her face. She could feel the curls against her fingers; the steam and dampness had taken her simple waves and made them go a bit crazy.

"This is a great spot," she said, leaning back to look at the stars that had popped out overhead. "I mean, I know this is supposed to be some great adventure tour, but I feel as if I'm in the lap of luxury. Wineries and great food and a massage and a soak in a hot tub. It's positively indulgent."

"Enjoy it now. In a few days we'll be roughing it."

"I know." While they were getting along so well, she decided to let him in on a little secret. "I've never been camping."

"Never?"

She shook her head.

"I went when I was a kid. Summer camps and stuff. I'm sure the gear here will be a little more high-tech than what I was used to."

"What were you used to?"

He looked over at her, his smile lazy. "Four of us crammed into a two-man tent with sleeping bags and pillows. No mats or air mattresses. But it might have been the best time of my life."

"Really?"

"Except for the time we were clearing out and we found a huge spider in the tent. Our camp leader came in and sprayed the heck out of it with bug spray. The thing was coated in white foam and it still didn't die for a good five minutes." He gave a shudder. "I'm not saying I'm wimpy about spiders, but that thing was huge."

Her eyes were feeling rather huge at the

moment as she stared at him. "Um...are there big spiders here?" she asked.

"Nothing poisonous, I don't think. Sorry. I didn't mean to freak you out."

"I'm not," she defended, determined to appear steady when inside she was picturing a spider in her tent and trying not to shudder at the thought.

But the mood had changed a bit, and Molly felt a bit off balance. She hadn't really been tested so far on this trip, and now she was afraid of looking silly in front of him as the more challenging aspects were just ahead. He seemed so...capable. Of anything.

"Just think, though," he said softly. "We'll be out there surrounded by nature, seeing orcas and sea lions and who knows what else? It's pretty amazing."

"I'm trying not to be intimidated."

"But you are?"

She nodded, deciding to confide a little. What would it hurt? That was the whole purpose of the trip, wasn't it? To stretch her boundaries a little? Besides, after this trip was over, she'd never see him again. There was some safety in that.

"I'm good at what I do, but I've lived a pretty sheltered life." Especially since Jack's death, when she'd been left an only child.

"I'm not used to feeling vulnerable. So while kayaking with killer whales sounds amazing and exciting, it's also way out of my comfort zone. I mean…" She gestured down at herself. "I'm this size. And an orca is…"

"Much, much bigger."

"I have this fear that one will swim under my kayak and flip me over."

"We'll stay close to shore. I don't think you have to worry about that."

"Probably not. But…it is what it is." She smiled weakly. "Please don't use that against me."

"I won't." He studied her with a somber expression. "I don't believe in using people's fears against them."

She thought about that for a moment. "Really? Because I'd think that might be a strategy for someone in acquisitions. A negotiating tactic."

He tilted his head as he thought for a minute. "No," he answered. "I might exploit a weakness, but not a fear. And, yes, there's a difference."

He removed one arm from the edge of the hot tub and turned to face her, only inches away. Her pulse hammered at her throat as his gaze captured hers. "What you just said? That's a fear." He moved an inch closer. "But the way I'm feeling right now, this close to you? That's a weakness."

Her breath caught. "Are you asking me to exploit it?"

His gaze dropped to her lips, then back up to her eyes. "Oh, it's tempting. Very tempting. But, no, not tonight."

She was surprised at the disappointment she felt at his words. His dark eyes held her captive for a long moment, while she pondered the wisdom of taking the single step forward. That was all it would take, really. One step and her lips could be on his. Her body brushing his, coming alive.

And then what? Up until this moment they hadn't even liked each other! And there was still the majority of the trip to get through, and if they kissed now and regretted it tomorrow, it would be awkward as hell. Because he would surely regret it, wouldn't he?

She swallowed. And he leaned back and said, "Good night, Molly."

Water splashed as he skirted around her and stepped out of the tub, steam rising off his lean body as he hit the cool outer air. Wordlessly, he grabbed his towel and briskly rubbed off most of the water before putting on his T-shirt and looping the towel around his neck.

"Good night," he repeated quietly and padded away.

Once he was gone she let out the breath she'd been holding and got out of the tub. Hot water slid off her suit and down her legs as she rushed to get her towel and robe.

He'd almost kissed her.

But at least he hadn't seen her in her bathing suit.

The woman had curves. Delicious ones that he had only glimpsed that day in the hotel room and last night in the hot tub. As Eric watched Molly pick her way across the gravelly shore toward inflatable boats, he realized that the last few days she'd worn clothing that did little to accentuate the dip of her waist and curve of her hips. The wet suit she was wearing, though—little was left to his imagination, and what *was* left was incredibly tempting.

He was attracted to her. He had come close to kissing her last night, which would have been a massive mistake. It was the spider, he realized. And the confession she'd made to him about being afraid. It had made him forget that he didn't like divorce lawyers and, right now, women in general.

Though that was hardly fair. Sure, he was

sour about the divorce, but if he were honest with himself, it wasn't all about the money. Not at all. He'd loved Murielle. Maybe not in the great love-of-a-lifetime way from the books and movies, but he had loved her and tried to show her in his way. It hadn't been enough.

She'd also made him pay, and she'd had a Molly on her side. He hadn't.

The tour guide, Shawn, nudged him. "You ready, Eric? Everyone's getting in the boats now. We'll head downriver a bit to the first pool and then get you in the water."

He climbed into one of the two boats— not the one Molly was in. He was looking forward to the trip, and the fresh air and the group's excitement scattered his heavy thoughts. Snorkeling was fun and today they'd be snorkeling with salmon. According to the tour information, tens of thousands of pink salmon returned to this river every year to spawn. They might even see some of the much larger but rarer Chinook salmon.

The ride in the boat was fun all on its own. The current of the river was fast, and they bounced along the waves while the summer sun beat down on Eric's head. They passed a pair of fly fishermen, who each lifted a hand in greeting, and went under a bridge that soared high above the river. It didn't take long and they slowed and put in to shore, where they would get in the water, put on their snorkel gear and be able to see what was happening beneath the surface.

"If anyone isn't up for snorkeling, they're welcome to stay in the boat and continue downriver with us," Shawn said, while the other guides helped sort out gear and gave instructions.

Eric looked over at Molly. For a moment she looked tempted, but then she reached for a mask and snorkel and slipped them over her head, a set to her jaw that was becoming familiar.

"Just a reminder to pair up as you go," Shawn called out. "The current will carry you downriver—you won't have to do much of anything. And the water's not overly deep. Relax and enjoy the view."

Eric made his way over to where she stood, alone on the bank. Once more the couples and groups were together and she was on the outside. "Need a buddy for the buddy system?"

She looked up at him and sighed. "Do you suppose we should just resign ourselves to the fact that we're going to be paired up because we're the odd ones out?"

He shrugged. "I can think of worse things. You're not so bad. For a divorce lawyer." In fact, he kept forgetting about that little tidbit more than he cared to admit.

She stifled a snort. "I guess you're okay. For an uptight businessman."

He laughed. "I know I'm uptight. It comes from being super focused. Believe it or not, you've seen me at my most relaxed."

"Me too. Pretty sad, isn't it?"

He was going to make a comment about how they'd both needed the trip, but they were interrupted by final instructions and then getting into the water. Molly stepped in beside him and they began to wade out. She stumbled on one of the round stones on the river bottom and reached out to grab his arm. Once she was steady she laughed and rolled her eyes.

"That wasn't intentional."

"I know you can't keep your hands off me."

She snorted then, and he laughed. Why was he bantering, flirting, if he wasn't interested in starting anything?

Maybe it was because this was a limited-time thing. When they'd first met they'd both been cranky and annoyed. But now…a vacation fling didn't seem like a half-bad idea. It would never go anywhere. He was used to weighing risks. This was fairly low-risk from where he was standing. Eight more days, then back to their own lives. No harm, no foul.

"Whatever keeps me from breaking my neck," she answered, letting go of his arm. "Priorities."

Self-preservation was a darn good priority. And one he wasn't exactly following at the moment. It wasn't just being thrown together because they were the odd ones out. There was something about her that drew him in.

"You ready?" He adjusted a setting on his wrist camera, and she tilted her head with curiosity.

"What's that?"

"An underwater wrist cam. I'm hoping to get some neat video."

"Boys and their toys," she muttered, but grinned up at him. He thought about maybe sharing some clips after the trip, but they probably wouldn't even speak again once it was over.

He was ready but she still hesitated. "What's wrong?"

She shook her head. "I'm fine. I've just never snorkeled before. I'm gearing myself up."

"If you can swim, you can snorkel. Just put your face in the water. Easy."

"Easy," she repeated, as if she didn't quite believe him. When he looked down, he saw her hands were shaking. But then she lowered her mask, put the snorkel in her mouth and slid into the water, putting her face in. Her personal flotation device kept her buoyant, and before he put his mask on he saw the tempting curve of her bottom break the surface. Lord, that wet suit was going to be the death of him today. He pulled down the mask and followed her into the water.

He put his face in and took a moment for his vision to adjust, and then he was entranced. The river bottom was alive. He turned his head and looked over at Molly, who was pointing ahead of him. When he tilted his head, he saw a school of salmon rushing past, darts of silver flashing in the sun-dappled water. They both stood and broke the surface at the same time.

"That's incredible!"

"Oh, my God, that's so cool!"

Then they both started laughing.

"This is really your first time?" he asked.

"I've always been too chicken on our family vacations. Instead I've done the glass-bottomed boat thing."

He wondered why a woman like her would choose to be on the outside rather than right in the middle of the action. "Well, we've got lots of day left. Let's go."

They spent the next thirty minutes in the water, the current carrying them forward as they explored the river. Occasionally they'd pop up and check their surroundings and the group; at one point they got back in the inflatable boats and headed downriver to a pool away from the rushing water. He could sense when Molly gained confidence and comfort; she moved through the water with greater ease and was quick to point out new schools of fish. They didn't see any of the famed Chinook salmon, but that was okay. Eric had had a blast, and by the smile on Molly's face when she peeled off her mask and snorkel, she had, too.

Her hair was wet and plastered awkwardly to her head, but her eyes were alight with excitement and her smile was wide and utterly genuine. He wasn't just entranced by the fish; there was something about her that made his stress and misgivings melt away. When was the last time he'd felt so free? He couldn't honestly remember.

They made their way back to the boats and he was tempted to climb in and sit beside her, just to remain close. Instead he chose the wiser course and moved to the second boat, making small talk with others. Despite his risk assessment, there was no way in hell he was going to trust his instincts when it came to romance right now. Heck, this wasn't even romance. It was elemental attraction. He was smart enough to realize it. And smart enough to recognize that he'd fallen into the same trap with Murielle. He'd got carried away and fallen too fast. By the time he'd realized it, it had been too late. There'd been a ring on his finger, and the weight of responsibility had fallen squarely on his shoulders. A man looked after his family, didn't he?

The boats started up the river and he stared over at Molly, her wet hair blowing back off her face and an ever-present smile on her lips. God. Maybe that was what really bothered him about the divorce. It wasn't that Murielle had called him a workaholic; he owned that. It was that she'd accused him of loving work more than he loved her, and she'd been wrong. Maybe he'd handled things the wrong way, but she'd made it sound as if there had never been any affection between them.

Of course, she'd said some other more hateful things, too. Like accusing him of being incapable of love at all. And then she'd hired a viper to rid him of thirty million.

Molly was one of those vipers. What would she say if she knew the real story behind his divorce? That it was 100 percent his fault?

CHAPTER FIVE

THE MORNING HAD been fun and exhausting, and then after a riverside picnic lunch, they'd gone to a museum in Campbell River for the balance of the afternoon. Molly had found the information and art about the coastal native peoples to be incredibly interesting and beautiful, but by five o'clock she was ready to pack it in, find a cool glass of white wine and call it a day.

Eric had moved on within the group and so had she; there was no need for partners during a group meal or wandering through the museum. She'd missed him, and that was enough of a warning sign. Snorkeling had been so amazing and fun. She'd always had this dreadful fear of breathing through the snorkel and going too deep and inhaling water. Just thinking about it brought back horrible, horrible memories from when she was a child. But pride had pushed her forward, and so had the current and her life jacket. Once she'd put her face in the water and had taken those first few breaths, she'd been fine, and thrilled at the sheer number of salmon in the river. Day one had indeed been an "easy" day of touring wineries. Today she felt as if she'd got her feet wet, both literally and figuratively. She'd conquered something that scared her, and it made her feel both strong and somehow lighter.

After a hot shower, she put on a pretty sundress and sandals and went to the patio bar, where she sipped on a glass of wine and let out a happy sigh. She was not sorry she'd come on the trip. Smiling, she took out her phone and scrolled through the pictures she'd taken today. One of Eric in the inflatable boat stood out. The wet suit clung to his physique and she swallowed tightly. There was no denying he took care of himself, if the breadth of his chest and shoulders was anything to go by. He'd had the wrist cam on and she wondered how his footage had turned out. And if—God forbid—she was in any of it, in her own very formfitting wet suit.

She took another drink of wine and felt defiance bubble up inside. Why shouldn't she put one on and do interesting and exciting things? Why should she let her insecurities hold her back?

Good Lord. She'd been wrapped up in Spanx and a power suit for so long that she wore it like armor. Instead of being protective, though, she was starting to see that her very appropriate dress and appropriate hair and appropriate shoes and apartment and social life were a prison keeping her from experiencing life.

She feared very much that she'd become the one thing that she'd been determined not to—a cookie cutter. Once, many years earlier, she'd fancied herself in love with an upperclassman. He'd been headed for big things, maybe even political aspirations, and she'd been the right sort of woman to have on his arm. But that was where he'd wanted her—on his arm. Not in law school, not in any position where, she realized now, she might have outshone him. When she'd announced she'd passed the bar, she'd expected him to propose. Instead he'd broken up with her.

He was the only man to have ever broken her heart, but she'd realized over time that it had been a lucky escape.

Except she hadn't really escaped at all. She'd still done what was expected of her and followed her father's wishes. The right office and the right cases and the right look—the family image. She was so tired of it. Tired of holding all the hopes and dreams of her parents because Jack had died.

Jack.

What would he say right now if he could? He'd been such a great kid, full of life and a laugh that never failed to make her smile. He'd teased her incessantly, and had also been determined to protect his little sister... Her throat tightened at the memory that she lived with every day.

She took another sip of wine and let the breeze through the evergreens soothe her soul. This distance from the life she'd built was good. She was starting to see she'd filled the role that Jack had been meant to play in the firm, but she'd forgotten to actually live for him, too. To experience things, like joy and adventure and wonder.

She stood up from the table and lifted her arms to the sky. There was a big world out there she had yet to experience, and she was going to live it, dammit!

Just as she was about to have a Kate Winslet–ish "gumption" moment à la *The Holiday*, her phone buzzed.

She didn't want to answer. It was her father again, and she let it go to voice mail, if nothing else but to prove a point. She was not on call. The office could survive without her for a couple of weeks.

It had taken being out of the country for her to realize how much she resented having toed the family line for so long. Did she even actually *enjoy* what she did for a living? Being at their beck and call day and night?

The phone buzzed again and she sighed, her earlier elation deflating. What if it was actually something important? Something to do with her folks or grandparents? She hit the button on the phone. "Hello?"

"Did you get my message?" Her dad's voice came through strong and clear.

"I didn't have time to listen to it. What's up?"

What followed was a five-minute update on the case he'd mentioned the day before. Molly gave up on trying to get a word in as he seemed determined to plow forward. When he finally took a breath, she stepped in with two words as she pressed her fingers to the top of her nose. "Dad. Stop."

The cool wine now seemed to fuel the beginnings of a headache. She took a deep breath and closed her eyes. "Dad, I'm on vacation. Since you can't seem to respect that, as I asked yesterday, I'm going to turn off my phone for the rest of my trip." Never mind that she was using her phone for a lot of her photos. There were ways around that.

"What is wrong with you?"

"Nothing. But there's more to life than the practice. I've always done everything you asked. Don't I deserve something for me?"

There was a pause. "I thought 'this' was what you wanted."

She knew he meant the job, the position, the lifestyle. And for a while it had been alluring. But most of all what she'd wanted was his approval. He always kept it just out of reach. Being made partner was great, but it came with a whole new set of expectations that she was never quite sure she could meet. Now she was taking a well-earned vacation and felt as if by doing so she was somehow letting him down.

"You never asked me what I wanted, Dad. It was assumed. I knew it was how I'd make you proud. That was what I really wanted." To make up for the son he'd lost.

Another long pause. Then her father cleared his throat. "So, about the case…"

Tears pricked the corners of Molly's eyes.

She never cried. But she'd been incredibly honest just now and her words were met with avoidance and rigidity. Because the Quinn family didn't talk about their feelings.

"I'm going to repeat what I said a few minutes ago, Dad, and this time I want you to really listen. I love you, but I'm on vacation. I'll be out of contact until my return in a week. As in, I'm not going to have my phone on." Her voice was clogged with emotion. She'd hardly ever gone against her father's wishes. Growing up, she'd idolized him. "I need this time to sort some things out. Please, please, let me have it." The longer she was away the more she realized how much she really didn't love her career, and her job took up the bulk of her waking hours. She was almost thirty and already having thoughts of "Is this all there is?"

"It's all yours," he answered, his voice slightly softer. "I hope you come to your senses."

She did, too, but she somehow thought they probably had differing definitions of what that meant.

She hung up and then turned off the phone, the final vibration humming against her palm before she put it down on the table. Then she jumped a little as another phone appeared beside hers, and Eric came to stand beside her chair. "Room for one more?" he asked softly.

She shouldn't be so glad to see him, but she was. She held out a hand, inviting him to take a seat. "I'm not sure I'm very good company," she said.

"Me either. I see you couldn't stay off yours, either." He nodded at the phones side by side on the glass table, and she sighed.

"It's off now. And isn't going back on again."

He smiled at her then. "Wouldn't it be fun to go down and chuck them into the ocean? I mean, really pull your arm back and let it fly?"

"Tempting, but then I'd be polluting the ocean."

"Are you always such a rule follower?"

She sighed. "Sadly, yes. You?"

"Not so much. Not that I actually break rules. Just that not everyone likes how I apply them."

"Ah. Because you're the bad guy who swoops in and takes over."

"I'm the bad guy who comes in and buys the business, straight up. I make good deals. People get upset because employees lose their jobs, but me buying the business helps create jobs somewhere else. The truth is, if the business had gone bankrupt, they would have lost their jobs anyway."

She looked at him for a moment and then laughed lightly. "You know, neither of us are in professions where people like us very much. Well, my clients like me, I suppose. And I'm sure your investors like you."

"Most of the time."

"Yes, most of the time."

And yet saying it made her feel a little bit sorry. She didn't have to be liked by everyone; she'd said goodbye to that long ago. But she might like to like herself a bit more, when all was said and done.

He leaned back in his chair and sighed. "We disassemble things, don't we, Molly? Break it up into pieces."

"Yeah."

He turned his head and looked over at her. "And we're both good at it. We've made a lot of money."

She nodded. "Yeah."

With his eyes locked with hers, he acknowledged, "I know why I'm so mad about the divorce. Or at least one of the reasons. Her lawyer did to me what I usually do with the businesses I buy. Except I wasn't the one who got the best deal."

That was what bothered him about the divorce? Losing?

She took a sip of wine and called him on it. "So you're mad about losing, but not about the end of the marriage?"

His gaze slid away and his expression darkened. "That's not what I meant."

"But it's what you said. I just… I guess I wonder if you really don't care that your marriage ended. If it's all about the thirty million."

Silence settled around them, warm and slightly uncomfortable in the summer evening. The breeze felt different here, smelled different from Cape Cod and the Atlantic somehow. It was wilder. More…primitive. Or perhaps that was just the setting. The river, the strait that ran between the island and the British Columbia coast and the rugged mountains made everything in Molly's life feel like it was half a world away.

"You're asking if I loved her," he said, and to her surprise his voice sounded a little hoarse.

"It's none of my business," she replied quickly. "I'm sorry I made it sound that way."

"I did," he confessed, and his dark gaze touched hers again. "But now that it's over, I'm starting to wonder if I don't actually know what love is. I just kind of know what it…isn't. I made mistakes, and I lost her."

Molly thought about her previous relationships since the "big breakup." They'd been practical and perfect on paper and… passionless. No heart involved, no hurt when it ended.

But didn't a girl deserve a little passion in her life?

She flipped her hair over her shoulder with her hand and felt the mellow breeze of the evening kiss her skin. "I'm not sure I know, either. But I know it's not on this phone." She tapped her nail on the phone cover and smiled. "I'm really starting to hate this thing."

"Me too."

Something rebellious began to bubble up inside her. "If we're not going to throw them in the ocean, what are we going to do with them?"

He looked at her, a sly smile making a small dimple pop in his cheek as his eyes warmed. "Wanna go for a walk?"

"I guess?" She wasn't quite sure what he had up his sleeve, but a summer walk with a handsome, sexy man wasn't a bad way to spend an evening. He got up from his chair and held out his hand, and she rose to take it. She was wearing sandals with her sundress, and hoped they were going to stay on the graveled paths around the lodge.

"Bring your phone," he said, and she picked it up and tucked it in the pocket of her skirt.

The sun was still out but was moving behind the mountains, casting shadows on them as they picked their way down the path toward the beach, a good half a kilometer away. The beach was actually a little cove tucked in along the Discovery Passage, running between the Strait of Georgia and the Johnstone Strait. Waves lapped against the shore and Molly kept her hand secured in Eric's, wary of tripping or stumbling on the uneven ground and rocks. When they got to the water, he let go of her hand and took a deep breath.

"This place is incredible, don't you think?"

She nodded. "I grew up on Cape Cod. It's different there. At home it's—"

"Inhabited." He nodded toward the water. "But here, it feels like there's not another person for miles around. I know there is, but it feels as if there isn't."

"It makes me feel small." She picked up a small rock and let it fly. It arced through the air before cutting into the water with barely a ripple. "Like that rock in a whole ocean floor."

"Do you always try to not make waves?" he asked, and it was a rather profound question when all was said and done.

"Yes," she answered honestly. "Hanging up on my dad was probably my biggest act of rebellion ever."

"Which is funny, because you strike me as incredibly competitive and competent. And stubborn."

She laughed. "I am. I have to be in my job. But not with my family."

"Why?"

It was a good question, and one she didn't want to talk about, not on the heels of her earlier thoughts. "How about you? What's your biggest act of rebellion?"

He accepted her evasion with a small smile. "Not going into business with my brothers."

"What do they do?"

"They run a car dealership."

"I see."

"Do you?" He turned his head to look at her. "Because I'm not sure they do. To them, I'm the guy who thinks they aren't good enough."

She picked up another rock and threw it

high into the air, watching it drop with a plop. "And do you think that?"

"No, of course not. It just didn't excite me, and I wanted to be excited. Challenged. Doing something new." He paused. "I wanted something with more security."

"Are you close with them?"

"Not anymore." She heard regret in his voice. She wondered if he was close with anyone.

"I'm sorry."

"It's not your fault. At least you're close with your family."

Am I? She wondered if she really was, or if the closeness was only because she had gone into the family business. What if she'd chosen another path? Would she be as close to her parents?

"I had a brother," she said, not sure what had prompted her to be so honest.

"Oh?" His dark eyes were keener now as they lit upon her. "Had. Past tense?" At her nod, he touched her shoulder. "I'm so sorry."

"I was five. Jack was ten. He was coming home from Little League with his best friend and his family when they were hit by a drunk driver."

"My God. That's horrible."

Her throat tightened. "I don't remember a

lot of it now. I was pretty small. But my family… Suddenly all their hopes and dreams for him transferred to me. There was a lot of pressure as the only child. I didn't want to disappoint them. And there was a lot of pressure to remember that I had chances and opportunities, whereas my brother's had all been taken away."

"You still have a right to your own life." She looked at him sharply, so he dropped his hand. "If that's what you want."

"I do. I just don't want to have the conversation." She reached inside her pocket for her phone. "I don't like what I do, Eric. I dole out the remains of what was once love and commitment. I look at it in terms of dollar signs and assets. God, do you know how awful it is when children are treated as assets? Or even family pets? To know that victory for my client means someone else is having their heart broken? Or that children are caught in the middle of a god-awful tug-of-war?"

She admitted something finally, in the fading light of a Pacific sunset, on the shores of a remote lodge with a handsome stranger. "I don't want to do this anymore. And I have no idea how to tell my family or what to do next."

He, too, took out his phone. "I'm all about the next deal, and time is always of the essence. Lost minutes can be lost thousands of dollars, even millions. And what do I have at the end of the day? More assets that I sell off to make more money, which I then invest in buying more assets. I'm very good at making money, Molly. But I suck at making anything that lasts. Including my marriage. The breakup was all my fault. Murielle probably would have worked at it if I had." He hesitated. "If I'd put as much effort into our emotional security as I did into our financial."

"Maybe...she just wasn't the right person. Because don't you think you'd have been there if she was?"

"I'd like to think that. But I'm not sure I can push the blame off on something as simplistic as 'not the right one.'"

Silence fell for a few moments, and then Molly brightened. "So, what are we going to do about this, then?" She shook her hand with the phone cradled in her palm.

He lifted his phone. "Maybe we need to make a ritualistic sacrifice."

"I thought we weren't going to throw them in the ocean."

"We're not. We're going to smash the hell out of them."

A laugh escaped her lips, an incredulous and delighted sound. "We are?"

"Yep." He looked around and found a somewhat flat rock. "Okay. We put them down here. We need another rock to smash them with."

"No one will be able to reach us."

"I left the name of the tour company. Did you?"

"Of course."

"Then they can reach us in an emergency. Are you in or are you out?"

Excitement rippled through her veins. Maybe this was a first step toward moving into her own independence. Choosing for herself.

She found a rock a little ways away, one that fit nicely into her hand, with a sharp edge on one side. "Will this do?"

"That looks perfect. Do you want to go first?"

"It's your idea. I think you should do the honors."

He took the rock and tossed it up and down in his hand a few times. "Okay. You ready?"

"If you are."

He put his phone down on the flat rock,

took a deep breath and brought his arm down in one swift swing. There was a crunching sound, and when he lifted the rock, his phone was shattered right in the middle.

"Okay, your turn."

Molly's insides churned. She wasn't sure why. It was just a stupid phone. It was nothing to be afraid of. She could buy a new one in the next town if she wanted.

He handed her the rock. She let it roll around in her hand for a moment, feeling the weight of it, the hard edges. Then she carefully set her phone down on the flat surface.

Then, with formidable strength and a steady aim, she brought the rock down on the screen and felt it shatter as the contact vibrated through her hand.

It did feel rather symbolic. And frightening. And liberating.

"You did it," Eric said approvingly. "I thought for a minute you were going to chicken out."

She shook her head. "Nope. It's time for a change. I think I've known it for a long time, and it took getting away for me to make the first step."

"Scared?"

"Plenty. But…" An expansive feeling filled

her chest. "But excited, too." She grinned up at him, thrilled when she saw him grinning back. "After today, I think everything is going to change."

CHAPTER SIX

She wasn't wrong.

Everything changed the next day, when they left Campbell River and headed farther north to their base camp on the Johnstone Strait. Civilization was left behind as they traveled to where they'd camp for three nights. Instead of taking full luggage, they took only what they'd need for their kayaking tour and left the rest at the hotel, where they'd return before heading on to other adventures.

It wasn't the sleeping-in-a-tent part that had Molly fazed. The tents were on platforms, and there were actual off-the-ground beds inside with plenty of comfortable bedding. No, it was the wobbly kayak in front of her that was freaking her out right now. This was far more daunting than the snorkeling, where she could put her feet down on the bottom of the river whenever she wanted and was only a few feet from shore, with a boat standing by.

"Bucket list," she reminded herself shakily. "Adventure doesn't mean it's easy. You got this, Quinn."

"Talking to yourself?"

"Yes." She looked up at Eric with a scowl. "I have a number of irrational fears, okay?"

"Don't we all?" He wiped his hands on his shorts. "Let me guess. Another first?"

"Yes." She huffed out a big breath. "And I'm afraid of tipping and…getting stuck underwater." The thought threatened to make her hyperventilate. She hadn't really thought it would be *this* hard.

He looked into her face by bending his knees a bit so they were the same height. "You'll bob right back up again."

"But these are the skinny kayaks," she said apprehensively. "I read that they're not as stable as the sit-on-top kind."

She knew she was not sounding very adventurous, so she straightened. "Never mind. I'll stop being a weenie."

She was a few steps away when he moved forward and caught her arm. "Not a weenie. But you're not the only first-timer here, and I'm sure the guides are used to it. Besides, like every other outing, you're not alone.

You'll be safe. The guides are with us, and we're with each other. Nothing's going to happen to you. Promise."

A strange look passed over his face, and she wondered why, but her nerves were jangling around too loudly for her to worry about it. He let go of her arm and went over to where his kayak waited. This evening they were going to learn the basics and paddle around their little cove as they got used to their kayaks. Tomorrow would take them farther up the strait. They'd be gone almost the whole day.

The instructor showed them how to get into the kayaks and adjust the skirt around the top to keep the water out of the cockpit. Molly felt less than graceful as she put one foot in and then the other, then got her feet positioned. She loved the *idea* of being on the water, but there was something about being secured that made her feel so vulnerable. Trapped. She had her paddle, and one by one the instructors came along and pushed each craft farther into the water until they were bobbing on the surface.

She had no idea why she felt as if the boat were on a tightrope or balance beam, but with each sideways movement she gave a gasp and then overcorrected.

One of the instructors pulled up alongside. "Nervous?"

"Very," she admitted.

The woman looked right in Molly's eyes. "You got this. The water's calm and you're not going to flip. I'm here, too."

It was exactly what Eric had said. Molly gave a quick nod. "Okay."

Once they were all bobbing, the instructors showed the correct paddling method, and they set off on little experimental lines in the immediate area. Molly looked over at Eric—his paddle sliced confidently through the surface of the water. She set her jaw and dipped her paddle, moving her shoulder and torso as she pushed the blade against the resistance of the water, then did the same on the other side. She shot forward, scaring herself but feeling a little exhilarated just the same. Over the next thirty minutes, she learned how to turn and back up, and the instructor even demonstrated a roll…in case someone capsized.

The nerves bubbled up again, making it hard to breathe.

Eric slid up beside her, his boat barely making a ripple in the water. "You look like you want to throw up," he said lightly.

But she shook her head. "Nope. I'm just

not going to need to know how to roll because I'm not going to capsize." She smiled brightly. "I didn't get to where I am today by letting stuff happen to me. I know how to take charge. I just need to put my mind to it."

Eric grinned. "Atta girl."

She rolled her eyes. "Please." She nudged away with her paddle. Maybe he didn't mean to be condescending, but it was time she faced up to those fears. If she couldn't handle a kayak, how was she going to handle telling her father she was leaving the firm?

Her body went cold. Was she really going to do that? Leave altogether? She knew she didn't have to decide today, but was she really leaning toward a full exit and on to something entirely different?

It was like being on a trapeze without a safety net.

She managed to paddle another half hour and then, after they'd put up their kayaks for the night, she changed into yoga pants and a light hoodie and joined the group around a blazing fire. The wood snapped and sparked as they talked quietly, but Molly rarely spoke, instead sitting with her thoughts. What did she want to do if she wasn't a part of the firm? Did she even still want to be a lawyer, or had that all been part of the expectations, too?

Eric showed up for about half an hour and then left again, and she was slightly relieved but more disappointed. He had a way of asking good questions and really making her think. Plus he was objective, wasn't he? Oddly enough, she found herself wanting his input and advice.

His words came back to her, from that first day at the winery. His wife—ex-wife—had called him "unavailable." Molly could see how that could be an accurate descriptor. He'd shared some things with her, sure, but he wasn't exactly an open book. And tonight, when they might have sat and talked around a blazing fire, he sat on the other side and then disappeared.

No, this was something she was going to have to figure out on her own.

And that wasn't a bad thing. Not at all.

The next morning dawned clear and mild. Sun streamed into Molly's tent and she stared up at the nylon ceiling for a moment, listening to the sounds around her, including the soft *lap, lap* of the waves on the shore of the inlet. Today was her biggest challenge yet: paddling with whales. It was nearly September, and their guide had said there was other wildlife they might encounter while on their trip. Humpbacks, bigger than orcas, were occasionally seen, and porpoises, seals and sea lions were all strong possibilities. Once more her stomach tumbled nervously, out of simple respect that she was so very small in comparison to the larger mammals. She closed her eyes and let out a breath. Eric had been right yesterday. She had to trust their guides. This was their job, and Molly didn't have to control everything.

She got up, dressed in yoga pants, a T-shirt and a light pullover and stepped outside her tent to start her day.

Breakfast was delicious and plentiful, and the group was full of barely concealed excitement for the day's journey. She didn't quite feel like eating and forced down as much as she could, as she'd be expending a lot of energy during the morning. Apparently they'd stop for lunch somewhere and then spend the afternoon coming back down the strait to base camp, dinner and a hot safari-style shower.

Before she was ready, they were at the shore, putting gear in dry bags and securing them in kayak compartments. For the first time, Molly regretted smashing her phone.

It was her camera for the trip, and now she had nothing. Maybe when they stopped at a town again she'd grab a cheap digital camera so she'd have it for the rest of her vacation.

Shawn, the main guide, came over and put his hand on her shoulder. "You look nervous. If you like, you can double up with me or with Eric. The double kayaks are a little more stable."

It was tempting, but her stubborn streak won out again. Yes, she had a terrible fear of being underwater, but she'd made it through snorkeling and she'd face this on her own, too. "I'll be okay," she assured him, more confidently than she felt. "I've got this. If you're patient, that is."

"Don't worry. We have several first-timers in the group. Nothing is rushed. That's not what the trip is about." He smiled at her. "If you need anything, just let one of us know. That's what we're here for."

He moved on and she glanced over at Eric, who was watching her. She gave a wave and a big smile, though the offer to partner up was incredibly tempting. At the end of the day she wanted to be able to say she did it. She wasn't worried about any of the other activities, but the snorkeling and kayaking were the two things that gave her pause. The idea of somehow being underwater and unable to breathe simply freaked her out. She'd been that way since she was a kid. She took a deep breath. Maybe she'd made safe choices all along because she knew what it was to be in over her head…literally.

Everyone got inside their kayaks, and before she could say "killer whales," she was in the water, clutching the paddle for dear life and semi-ready to face the challenge ahead.

They started out slowly, getting the hang of things and finding a rhythm with the paddles. Molly concentrated so hard she didn't have much of a chance to really look around her and take in the scenery, but she was more focused on staying upright and her technique than the rugged shoreline or the view of the mountains on the mainland in the distance.

About an hour into their trip they paused and watched a group of Dall's porpoises, their sleek forms arcing in and out as they raced through the water. Farther on they saw seals sunning themselves on rocks in the late-morning sun, a few of their little heads poking through the water, their dark eyes full of mischief. Molly got a little thrill as one adventurous seal followed along beside her kayak for a while. She wondered if the seal was curious or even somehow challenging her to a race, but after five minutes or so it disappeared beneath the surface and its little head popped up several meters away. They stopped for lunch and feasted on thick sandwiches, salad and iced tea, then took some time to sit on the rocks and chill out.

This was the most beautiful place Molly had ever seen. Not another person for miles. Not a house or a store or anything—it was untouched. She thought of her place back home, and all the day-to-day concerns that ate up her time. How many of them really mattered? They didn't. Not here. And it made her crave a simpler life.

It also gave her some much-needed clarity.

She looked over at Eric. He was so handsome, so charismatic. The man who'd barged into her hotel bathroom in Victoria wasn't the real Eric Chambault. Eric was genuine and smart and funny. So what if he didn't spill his guts every second? They were strangers, after all. When all was said and done, he'd actually shared a lot, and had given her a boost of confidence on more than one occasion. Not to mention making her toes curl at their near kiss in the hot tub. She couldn't deny that he was in her thoughts in ways that weren't entirely innocent. What would happen if they kissed? Did she really want to go there? Wouldn't it just complicate things?

And was it possible to have a holiday fling without feelings being involved? Because she was self-aware enough to know that she was vulnerable right now, being at a personal crossroads. And the last thing she needed was to be hurt because she'd set up expectations that could never be met.

She'd expected her ex to be supportive, after all. And he wasn't. He hadn't cared about her dreams. His definition of love had meant having the right sort of wife on his arm for his own ambitions. What did she expect out of Eric? Anything?

He looked over and met her gaze, and the moment held longer than was polite. Recognition and heat flashed in his eyes, and Molly's cheeks flushed though she didn't break eye contact. The near kiss in the hot tub had been so close that she'd almost felt his lips against hers. What would it be like to actually be touched by him? To be kissed for real and held in his arms?

He lifted an eyebrow and she couldn't help it; her lips twitched in a saucy curve. Lord, she loved how he challenged her. She was braver when he was around, and she liked that about herself.

Shortly after that they were back in their kayaks and heading south again, toward base camp. Little islands dotted the strait, and the guides took them on a slightly different route. Paddling was a little more effortless, and Molly started enjoying the ride. They were only half a kilometer from camp when a shout went up and a ripple of excitement raced through the group.

A pod of orcas, their dorsal fins straight and black, broke the surface, maybe a hundred and fifty meters away.

Restrictions prevented the group from getting any closer. It didn't, however, prevent the killer whales from coming closer on their own. The tour group stayed close to the shoreline of the little island, and before long the whales were only about fifty meters away, curving through the surface, black-and-white and startlingly large. The closer they got, the more excited and anxious Molly became.

One particularly active one broke the surface and there was a loud sound as water and air rushed out of its blowhole. Behind it, three more surfaced, coming ever closer.

This was exciting, but from a distance. Molly's fear of a whale getting too close to her little kayak took hold again, and her hands trembled on her paddle. She put the blade in the water and tried to move to the inside of the group, but the waves were lapping around the fiberglass and she was too inexperienced to maneuver well. She froze when she could see the white circle on the head of the lead whale, the height of the dorsal fin so large this close-up. It went under the water again and she imagined it heading straight for them, beneath their kayaks. What would happen if it tried to surface and they were in the way?

She stuck her paddle in the water and pushed, but had the blade the wrong way and only succeeded in turning herself sideways. Then when she leaned forward to compensate, she felt the boat shift. Once more she threw her weight to the side, and that was when it happened. Over she went, under the water, her feet in the cockpit of the kayak, the skirting tucked around her and the image of a three-ton mammal passing below her lodged in her brain.

She began to flail, but the boat didn't right itself.

It was hard to hold her breath when panic filled her chest. If she couldn't get flipped back over, she would open her mouth and take in water and drown. Or she'd get

bumped by the whale and injured and—
OMG, OMG, OMG…

Suddenly she was pulled out of the water, the kayak righted, and Shawn had a firm grip on her life jacket. "Breathe," he commanded. "You're okay."

But she wasn't. Inside she was falling apart.

Everyone was looking at her and she couldn't even put on a mask to show she was all right. She shook all over. She was wet and her legs were stiff and she couldn't breathe.

Shawn still held her jacket. "I've got you. You're okay. Bend forward and breathe as deeply as you can. You're okay."

She hadn't had a panic attack since eighth grade, but the feeling was familiar and terrifying. Gray spots floated in front of her eyes as she tried and failed to slow her breath, and the muscles in her legs twitched but wouldn't release. She was right-side up but she could still picture the whale going under and where was it now and…

"Slow, deep breaths. You're fine. We're all fine. Nothing is going to happen now. Just take your time, listen to my voice and know that it's going to be all right."

Eric's deep voice came from beside her, and two tears slid down her cheeks. She still had her head down, so she knew he couldn't see them, but her relief at hearing his voice was profound.

"Where did they go?"

He knew exactly what she meant. "They're out farther now. You're okay. Everyone's okay." He reached for one of her hands and settled it between his. "Keep breathing."

The touch of his fingers on her hand was a lifeline. She didn't know where Shawn had gone but that was okay. Slowly her breathing eased and the cramp in her lungs abated. The gray spots disappeared from her vision and she lifted her head, feeling fragile but no longer like she was going to pass out.

And embarrassed. So very embarrassed.

"There you are," he said quietly. "Better?"

She nodded. "Feel stupid."

He smiled softly and shrugged. "No one's perfect."

But she was supposed to be. Since she was five, she'd followed instructions. Done what was expected. Then these things didn't happen. Even as she thought it, she realized how impossible it sounded. Real life wasn't like that.

"After years of thinking I had to be, it's a tough adjustment," she replied, wishing she could get her legs out of the cockpit and massage the muscles that had cramped.

It was only then that she realized Shawn was still beside them. "Molly, we can pull in and switch some pairings around so you're in a double for the rest of the way back to camp. You might be more comfortable with that."

And more conspicuous, and what a pain when they were this close to being "home."

"I can do it," she said, her voice sounding more confident than she felt. "It's not far. I can see the camp from here." Not well, but she could see the cookshack structure and the faint dots of the colored tents through the trees.

"You're sure?"

"I'll paddle beside you," Eric said. "Like a wingman."

She wasn't about to refuse that offer. "Okay," she answered, and Shawn handed her the paddle that she'd let go of when she'd capsized.

The group was rather quiet as they made their way back to camp, and once they were on the shore, several people came to check on her, which made her feel both foolish and also cared for. She told each that she was fine, but what she really wanted was to go to her tent and decompress. Change into dry clothes and figure out what the heck was wrong with her.

Eric hovered, and she needed him to not. Because if she was going to fall apart again, she wanted to do it in private.

"I'm going to change," she said to him, not quite meeting his gaze. "I'm wet and I'm going to be cold in this wind if I don't get into something dry."

"Of course. You're okay?"

"I'm fine. I'll see you at dinner."

She made her way to her tent and quickly changed out of her wet clothes into dry ones, including a fleece-lined sweater that she'd brought along for cooler nights. A woman's voice outside asked if she wanted first crack at the shower, which she gratefully took, even though showering outside was a bit of an adventure in itself and out of her comfort zone. She went back to her tent and hung up her clothes to dry, and then it was time to gather for dinner. All the while she went through the motions, avoiding thinking too much about the panic attack and what had caused it. As far as the group went, they'd all see Molly smiling and perfectly fine after the incident. Because that was what she wanted them to see.

She went to bed early, hoping to sleep off the last dregs of adrenaline. She slept right in her leggings and sweater, tucked into her sleeping bag on the camp mattress. It took a while for her to drift off, but her body was so exhausted from the day of paddling and the rush of the panic attack that she finally closed her eyes and fell into slumber.

CHAPTER SEVEN

ERIC COULDN'T SLEEP.

He kept seeing Molly's face over and over in his mind. He'd watched her flip, then started paddling closer as Shawn had expertly helped her right-side up. But the sheer panic and fear was etched on his brain. He remembered that look, the shallow breathing and the inability to think straight. Seeing Molly go through it brought it all back to him, when he'd been a boy and helpless to help his mother deal with the grief and stress of being abandoned.

Molly had paddled the rest of the way back on her own, and he was damn proud of her for that. And she'd changed, gone to dinner, eaten. And yet somehow he got the impression that she had been just going through the motions. That she wasn't as okay as she seemed.

He turned over onto his side and let out a

sigh. When closing his eyes seemed impossible, he got up and quietly exited his tent, using a small flashlight to make his way to her platform. He just wanted to check to see if she was all right. Everyone else here had a partner. They weren't alone. She was. And today she'd been deathly afraid.

He got to her tent and clicked off his light, not wanting to wake her if she actually had managed to go to sleep. He waited a few minutes, pleased when nothing but silence came from within. And he was just about ready to turn away when an odd sound came from inside.

He froze, listening harder. The sound got louder, too. A strangled, choking sound and fast breathing. A thump as if something had hit the wooden bed frame. Heart in his throat, he stepped up to the zippered door.

"Molly?"

Another groan and cough and he spoke a little louder. "Molly? Are you okay?"

Abrupt silence, then a forced "I'm fine."

And he might have believed her if she hadn't had this little hiccup at the end that told him she was crying.

"I'm coming in." He unzipped the door and stepped inside. It was still dark, so he clicked on his light again but turned it toward the floor, so the light wasn't directly in her face. He could see her eyes, though, huge and luminous in the pale light. Her face was streaked with tears, which she scrubbed away quickly.

He went to her side and sat on the edge of her bed. "Nightmare?" he asked softly.

She nodded, let out a deep breath.

"You're not panicking now, though. That's good."

"My heart's beating out of my chest."

He was tempted to see if it was true, but touching her right now would be wrong. Not when she was vulnerable and scared. And yet he couldn't do nothing. He reached out and wiped some moisture off her cheek with his thumb. "You held up like a champ all evening. But when we sleep, our barriers are down."

She nodded. "Yeah. I'm sorry. You should go back to bed."

"Not until I make sure you're all right. The dream sounded rough."

A mortified expression swept over her face. "Oh, God. Do you think anyone else heard?"

He shook his head. "I couldn't sleep and came over to check on you. It was all quiet until just before I came in." They were talking in low voices, barely over a whisper. "I wanted to wake you before it got too bad."

Her exhalation was shaky. "It was bad enough. There's something that's been bothering me for so long. My thing with snorkeling and the flipping over—it all has to do with being underwater and not being able to breathe. All my life I stuck to swimming pools, to wading at the beach but not really swimming, doing the boat thing instead of snorkeling on family vacays and just telling myself it was a preference and I wasn't really afraid. As much as I've tried to block it out or rationalize it away, it's still there. It's not a dream. It's a memory."

"What happened?"

"I got caught in a riptide at the beach and couldn't get back to shore. A wave came and I went under, and I couldn't shout, and I didn't think anyone noticed. I had to fight so hard to get back to the surface again. I knew I was going to drown."

"How old were you?"

"Five."

Five years old and afraid of drowning. "It would explain a lot. Then what happened?"

"I was rescued. My brother rescued me, because he was already a strong swimmer and I hadn't stayed close to the shore like I promised." She shuddered all over. "I can still feel the water pulling me under, and coughing when I bobbed up again. Today… the whales were getting so close. And one went under and I tried to move to get farther away and then everything went…*hinky* and I ended up upside down. I couldn't get turned around and all I could think of was what if the whale was beneath me and my head was right there…"

Her breath was coming fast again. "I know it sounds ridiculous—"

"But the fear is real," he said, finishing for her. "Doesn't matter if it's rational or not. Fear is fear. I'm so sorry, Molly."

"It's not your fault. I'm just so glad you were there. You knew exactly what I needed to start breathing again."

He rubbed his hand over hers. "Well, it's not my first experience with panic attacks. My mom had them for a while after my dad left. I think dealing with everything as well as raising three boys took its toll." He thought back to those days and felt a pang of regret. He hadn't always been the easiest kid to raise. "When Mom had one, I learned not to hug because it was too confining and claustrophobic. But she liked a point of contact, so a hand on her arm or leg let her know someone was there. And for me to talk to her."

"That's rough on a kid."

Not as rough as losing his father had been, but he simply shrugged. "She's my mom. I love her. I could be a real handful, but I'm also the oldest. My brothers called me the Golden Boy." He grinned a little. "They weren't really wrong."

"You looked after her."

"I tried. My dad...he got into a lot of debt and then took off, leaving my mom to clean up his mess and with three boys to raise. I tried to step up and do whatever I could to help."

He still did. His mom wouldn't take a lot of his money, but at least she lived mortgage-free now, in a tidy little bungalow rather than the house where they'd grown up. His brothers made sure she had decent wheels through the dealership. Materially she was in good shape. But he missed her. Their relationship had become strained, too.

They sat for a few more minutes before Eric asked, "Are you feeling better now?"

"Yes, thanks."

She said the words, but he wasn't quite convinced. There was a hesitation to them that told him she wasn't okay but wouldn't ask for help. "Are you really? Or are you afraid of having the nightmare again?"

She laughed nervously. "Am I that transparent?"

"Yes." And then he chuckled, and she laughed a little in return, the soft sound reaching in and waking something in him that had been dormant a long time.

He got up and as carefully as possible moved the empty bed in the tent over, so it was right up next to hers. He didn't have his sleeping bag, but he didn't care. He lay down on the mattress and shifted to his side, facing her. "Is this okay? I promise I'll stay on my side. But you won't have to be alone."

"You don't have any covers."

"I'm in sweats and a hoodie. I'm fine."

She rolled to her side. He'd turned off his light and the tent was pitch-black, so he could barely even make out her form in the darkness. It lent an intimacy to the moment that made his breath catch in his throat.

She reached out and touched his arm, then followed his arm down to his wrist and then hand, twining her fingers with his. "Thank you, Eric. For helping me today. For being here tonight."

"My pleasure," he replied gruffly.

He'd been married to Murielle for six

years. Dated her for two before that, after meeting her through mutual friends. He'd been a typical guy in college and he'd dated as much as anyone. But this sweet interaction affected him as deeply as any of his previous relationships, including his marriage. And he'd known Molly less than a week. How could that be?

He stayed awake until Molly's breathing evened out and the grip on his hand eased. Then he finally drifted off to sleep.

When Molly woke, she discovered Eric snuggled tightly against her on the single bed, the second bed he'd pulled over next to hers now empty. He was still outside her sleeping bag, dressed in his sweats and hoodie, but he must have got cold in the night and moved closer for body heat.

Not that she was complaining. His arm was draped over her ribs possessively, his thighs next to hers. It had been a long, long time since she'd awakened next to a man, and it made her want to move closer. To unzip the sleeping bag and remove some of the barriers between them.

It also made her think of the night before, and the horrible nightmare, and how he'd been there to hold her hand and talk her through it. Just as bad as the near drowning, had been remembering the rescue. How unfair that she'd been saved only two months before Jack had been taken from them.

Eric sighed in his sleep and tenderness washed over her. He wasn't just incredibly sexy; he was a good man underneath. The story about how he'd helped his mother after his dad had left said a lot about the man he was.

Morning light filtered through the fabric of the tent, and when Molly shifted a little, Eric's eyelids fluttered open. They met hers for a moment, and her heart gave a solid *whomp* against her ribs at the connection that flowed between them. She liked him, sure, but there was also this elemental attraction that she kept trying to ignore but refused to be locked away. He lifted his hand and put it against her cheek and she closed her eyes for a moment, lost in the tenderness of the touch.

"Did you sleep?" he asked, his voice rough from disuse.

She nodded. "Much better, after…"

A small smile curved his lips. "Sorry about the close quarters. I got cold."

"You didn't need to stay," she said, though she was incredibly glad he had.

"Yeah, I did." He moved his hand off her

ribs, and she suddenly felt a little bit cool from the lack of contact and the weight of his palm on her sleeping bag.

"Well, thank you. I slept better with you here, for sure. No more nightmares."

"That's good." They were practically whispering, even though there wasn't a sound from the other campers. "I should go, though. Because, you know."

"Because someone might see you leaving my tent?"

"Yeah. That." He smiled wider. "We keep telling people there's nothing going on, but…"

"Yeah. We seem to keep ending up together."

Eric leaned forward and, to her great surprise, kissed her forehead. "I'm gonna go before I do give them something to talk about. Are you okay to paddle today?"

She wasn't, but she'd figure it out. She also knew the important thing was to get back in the boat. "I'll be fine."

"Okay. I'll see you at breakfast."

He slid off the bed and stood, then stretched, moving his arms out to the side instead of up in the air, where they would have touched the top of the tent dome. Then with a wink, he slipped into his sandals, un-zipped the flap and disappeared.

Molly flipped to her back and stared at the ceiling. There was something going on between them, and it wasn't just friendship and comfort. The big question was, what did she want to do about it? And were they possibly on the same page?

They avoided making eye contact during breakfast, but when they arrived on the beach to get ready for the day's trip, Shawn approached. "Hey, you two. I thought maybe today you'd like to go in a two-seater. It's a little more stable and we were thinking it might make you a little more comfortable, Molly."

She hoped she wasn't blushing. Still, why should she? Why did it matter what people thought? So what if she and Eric had struck up a…friendship on this trip? Courtroom confidence was one thing, but when was she going to be more self-assured in her personal life?

She thought back to attending the benefit with Ryan and how she'd found it very easy to turn down any offers of more than friendship. She'd had no problems with self-assurance then. So maybe it was Eric. Maybe it was him plus the discovery that she was going to be making a life change that had her all discombobulated.

But once again, her brain asked, *Who cares?*

She nodded. "If it's okay with Eric, I don't mind."

"Fine by me," Eric said with an easy smile.

Shawn left them and Eric looked over at her as he was slipping on his life vest. "Do you want the front or back?"

Molly didn't really know, so she shrugged. "How about we go one way up the sound and reverse it on the way back?"

"Works for me. I'll go front first?"

"Sure."

They got their kayak to the water's edge, and Eric turned around. "I'm glad we're together today."

"Me too."

"Molly?"

She stopped adjusting her PFD and looked up at him.

"Not just because of your nervousness, okay? I'm glad to be with *you.*"

It didn't matter that last night had been as chaste as they came. Something had changed, and it took away the nerves of being on the water and replaced them with something deliciously anticipatory.

The morning passed without event; the weather was beautiful and the scenery as gorgeous as before, and they took a slightly different route along the sound. Still, other than a few seals and a ton of bald eagles, they reached the previous day's stopping point without encountering any whales or dolphins. Paddling was more fun with two once Molly found her rhythm with Eric, and he often turned around to say something or would point toward a neat tree or a bird circling above. They carried on for nearly an hour before one of the guides indicated that something was nearby. Molly peered through her sunglasses to see, but there was nothing. As they drew closer to the group, she heard the word *humpback* and more excited chatter about *bubbles*.

"What's going on?" she asked, knowing Eric would hear her.

"I think they've spotted some humpbacks," he replied, excitement in his voice.

Molly tried to quell the nerves in her stomach. Humpbacks were way bigger than orcas, but yesterday had shown her that the biggest threat to her was her own panic. She kept her eyes trained on the place where people were pointing, glad she and Eric were in the kayak together.

One of the guides' voices broke through. "If you look, you'll see the bubbles on the surface, what looks a bit like a rolling boil, if you're into cooking terms. The humpbacks use 'bubble net' feeding to corral the fish into one spot and then they can all feed. Hold on, because it's going to get exciting."

It felt as if the whole group was holding its breath, as anticipation was rife in the air. When the whales plunged to the surface, everyone jumped a little and exclaimed in excitement. Molly was no exception. It was incredible! She couldn't tell how many whales there were, but the waves made by their forceful break of the surface were significant. Eric had his camera out and was snapping wildly. Molly simply took in the sight and tried to ignore the anxiety that still beckoned. She could do this. She was doing it!

They watched the feeding ritual for a good twenty minutes, before the humpbacks moved on with a signature wave of their flukes. Around two hundred meters away or so, one breached the surface and then crashed down again in a magnificent show of force and beauty. As their group continued on, the chatter increased significantly as everyone marveled at what they'd seen. They didn't travel far before they encountered a group of sea lions, basking in the sun on the rocky shore. One or two bobbed around in the water, but the rest were soaking up the rays. As they paused to watch and the guides gave them the lowdown on the species, two of the sea lions started a conversation that had Molly laughing. The groans and growls sounded so grouchy that she couldn't help but giggle, and before long she heard Eric's low chuckle as well.

"Is that what your clients sound like?" he asked, still laughing.

"Not usually. Most of the time my clients don't speak to each other," she replied, then sighed. "How about you and your wife? Did your marriage go out with a whimper or a bang?"

His smile faded, and though she couldn't see his eyes because of his sunglasses, she imagined the light went out of them, too, and she felt sorry she'd asked the question so flippantly. "A whimper. I wasn't angry. Not at the divorce, really. We weren't happy. I was angry about *that*."

"That you were unhappy?"

"Yeah. I worked pretty hard to set up the perfect life, so why wasn't I happy?"

She let out a mirthless huff of air. "If you

figure that one out, let me know. I'm the girl who has everything and is unhappy with it. I suppose that makes me ungrateful."

"Not necessarily. Don't be so hard on yourself."

"Maybe you should take your own advice."

They began paddling again, moving past the sea lions and onward to the stopping point for lunch. After two days of paddling, Molly's shoulders and back were aching and she was ready for a good stretch. Eric got out of the kayak first, and then held out his hand to help her out. She took it and felt the warmth of his hand through the fabric of her paddling gloves—he held her fingers a little longer than was necessary.

She could get used to him looking at her this way.

But she dropped her hand from his, and once they'd secured the kayak, they headed up the bank to the picnic area.

The way home was even better, with Molly's confidence growing as they paddled down the strait toward base camp again. The orcas were absent this afternoon, but Molly didn't care. She dipped her paddle in and out of the water in time with Eric, who was now in the back. The breeze blew her hair off her face and she couldn't ever remember feeling this alive. By the time they'd reached "home," she was sad to leave the kayaking behind. Two and a half days hardly seemed long enough. Tomorrow morning's expedition was a boat ride farther up the strait on a quest to see grizzly bears, and then it was back to the lodge and luxury before the next leg of their journey. She was sorry this part was over just as she was getting comfortable with it.

She and Eric sat together over dinner and chatted with others while dining on fresh cedar-planked salmon, baby potatoes and salad. Food even tasted better outdoors, she decided, and when the evening was waning she and Eric went for a walk on the beach. The moon was out and stars peeked from their inky blanket, giving the couple enough light to see where they were going.

Eric reached over and took her hand. After they'd walked a good distance, he led her to a large rock pushed up against the grassy overhang. They were hidden from camp, but the beach and the cove stretched out before them. The air tasted like salt and evergreens.

He climbed up and then helped her up, until they were settled in the natural seat of the boulder. He put his arm around her and snuggled her in, then let out a deep, satisfied sigh.

She understood. She was feeling the same way right now, and was afraid that saying anything would break the perfect moment.

So they sat in the silence for a long time, listening to the sounds of the water, the soft *shhh* of unseen wildlife nearby—squirrels, perhaps, or something equally innocuous. Laughter came from the area of the campfire, making a smile bloom on Molly's face.

She'd always been a city girl. Not much into roughing it or spending loads of time in nature, at least not more than the local park or gardens. But this was perfection. Bidding on this trip had been on a whim, but it was turning out to be the best decision of her life.

"What are you thinking?" he asked. "I can hear the wheels turning in there."

"That I wish I'd done this sooner."

"Me too. But then, we wouldn't have met. And despite our inauspicious beginning, I'm finding I'm glad we did."

"Yeah," she whispered, burrowing into his embrace a little deeper.

They sat a while longer, long enough that a shooting star swept across the sky. "So," she whispered. Speaking in a regular voice seemed harsh, somehow, as if the evening required hushed tones and a bit of reverence. "As of tomorrow, we're halfway through our trip."

"I know."

"And then we'll both be going back to our own lives."

"We will."

"And I'll be in Boston and you'll be in Montreal, or wherever your work is going to take you once this is over."

"I suppose you're right." There was a pause, and then he said, "You're wondering if it's worth exploring this." She didn't have to ask what "this" was; they both knew it was the attraction humming between them. "If it's a good idea. What'll happen when it's over and we have to go our separate ways."

She nodded, her ponytail rubbing against his chest.

His lips touched the hair beside her ear. "We have to go back to our lives. We both know that."

His warm breath on her hair sent delicious shivers down her spine. "Yes," she agreed, feeling a little breathless. "Back to our lives." Even if she suspected her life was going to change a bit. It was odd not knowing what it would look like, but that wasn't a thought for this moment. Not for tonight.

"So no expectations," he murmured, his lips still close to her ear, his hand on the curve of her waist. "Just…"

She turned her head a little, leaning into him so his lips grazed her temple and sent a thrill zinging down to her toes. "Just being in the moment," she said, finishing his thought. Her lips remained slightly open as they made cautious movements—a touch here, a press of the lips there. They were prolonging the anticipation but not fighting it—not anymore. She turned into him, so that she was cradled in his left arm as her face turned up to his. The look in his eyes was hungry and she bit down on her lip as her lashes fluttered a little. She was dying for him to finally kiss her on the mouth. When he did, she lifted her arm and curled her hand around his neck, drawing him down so he was half on top of her, sandwiched between the cool rock and the warm, sexy man who was currently tasting her lips so expertly she would swear she heard music.

He lifted his head, his mouth only a few inches from hers, his gaze burning down into her. She hadn't been wrong—she did hear music. Up by the campfire. One of the guides must have brought a guitar, and a couple of voices joined in.

Molly was swamped with a sense of the surreal, but she let it sweep her away. This was a once-in-a-lifetime trip. A once-in-a-lifetime opportunity. She wasn't going to squander it.

She pushed up with her hands and saw Eric's face blank with surprise as he sat upright and she straddled him, a knee on either side of his hips. The closeness had her body humming in response, and she put her hands on his face and kissed him, taking the lead and loving every moment of it. His arms came around her and pulled her close, one hand skimming down her ribs as his thumb grazed the side of her breast. She felt so *alive*. So free.

Eric slid his mouth away from hers and kissed her collarbone, his hot breath radiating through the cotton of her shirt. For a moment she allowed herself to fantasize about making love here, on a rock beside the water, with the sound of the waves ebbing and flowing around them. It would be so good. But there were also ten other guests and three guides not far away, and the inconvenient realization that she had no protection. This possibility had never crossed her mind.

"I don't have anything. Do you?" she

asked, unsure which answer she truly wanted him to give.

"No." He stopped moving and lifted his head away from the vee of her shirt. "Dammit."

She laughed a little, the sound rich and full of promises that weren't to be fulfilled—at least not tonight. "It's okay. It's like Christmas. All the fun is in the lead-up."

"Yeah, except at Christmas you're pretty sure Santa's going to come at some point."

She burst out laughing, the sound echoing down the beach as she slapped her hand over her mouth. Eric was watching her with an amused expression, though he seemed a bit sheepish.

"We should get back," she said, though she was disappointed at having to say it. "It's getting late and tomorrow's another early morning."

"Are you going to sleep all right? You did much better today."

She nodded. "I still had some anxiety, but not the all-out panic. I kept reminding myself that I wasn't alone, and that my biggest enemy was my own fear and not any actual threat. It helped."

He nodded. "Well, tomorrow it's safe and sound in the boat. And then back to the hotel."

His gaze met hers. The hotel meant hotel rooms. Amenities. Opportunities to pick up contraception.

"Back to the hotel," she echoed.

The thought seemed to spur them both into action, and they hopped down from the boulder and made their way back up the beach. But Eric reached down and held her hand.

It was the best feeling in the world.

CHAPTER EIGHT

ERIC STEPPED OUT of the hot shower and grabbed a thick, fluffy towel from the warming rack. It was so good to be back in the hotel, with a real mattress and electricity and hot running water on demand.

Though he could honestly say he'd enjoyed the kayaking trip immensely. After all, he'd seen orcas. Humpbacks. Sea lions, seals, eagles and grizzlies on the final day during a fun boat ride. And he'd kissed Molly. That part left him happy and yet unsatisfied. It had been tamer than 90 percent of his make-out sessions as a teenager, but it had been amazing, too.

And now they were back in Campbell River, in the lap of luxury, in a hotel with a small gift shop that carried condoms. If it didn't happen, it wouldn't be because neither of them were prepared.

And he wanted it to happen. Her flip into

the water and subsequent nightmare had awakened all his protective instincts. He frowned a little as he looked in the bathroom mirror. Molly was an independent, successful woman. She didn't really need him in a material sense, but he got the feeling she did in an emotional and physical sense. His stomach plummeted. Was that what Murielle had been saying all along, and he was too stubborn to see it? Had she really wanted him and not the financial security he could provide? He'd spent so many years ensuring those he cared about had enough—a place to live, food on the table. What if he'd got that wrong?

He didn't dare dwell on that tonight, so after he'd shaved, he pulled on a pair of jeans and a soft cotton shirt, doing up the buttons while thinking about the night ahead. Molly had said that she was going to get a massage and then have a hot bath before dinner, and he'd asked her to join him for the meal. Not with the group, but just the two of them, at their own table. There'd been a moment of hesitation, and then she'd smiled and said yes. The tour group already assumed they had coupled up; it was evident in the assessing yet friendly looks and the way they were often paired together in conversation.

And who gave a damn about appearances, anyway?

He had, for a long time. But not now. At least not at this moment.

At the appointed hour he went to her room and knocked on her door. She opened it and for a moment he was speechless. She looked…amazing. Her dress was deep red and wrapped around her body with a tie at her left hip, so that the vee of the neckline hinted at her cleavage and the fabric draped over the curve of her hips. She wore heels, which put her only an inch or so shorter than him, and her hair… She'd done something with it to make it all curly, and then twisted it up somehow in the back, revealing the elegant column of her neck. And she wore makeup tonight, more than he'd seen her wear before. Her eyes glowed and her lips were plump and shiny…and he had the thought that maybe they could skip dinner altogether. He'd loved her figure in her go-to yoga pants and tops on the kayak trip, but right now she was a flat-out bombshell.

"Wow," he said, swallowing hard, thinking he sounded like an idiot. All those thoughts and all he could get out of his mouth was "wow"?

"I wanted to dress up," she said softly, reaching for her purse. "You don't mind?"

"Are you kidding? Except I feel incredibly underdressed." He should have at least put on a tie.

"Not at all. You look…"

She hesitated, and despite the makeup, her cheeks colored.

"I look what?" he asked, wanting to hear her say it. He didn't know if tonight was going to be foreplay or torture but he was willing to go along with it and find out.

"You look nice," she said, stepping out of the room and shutting the door.

But he touched her arm and stood in front of her, so that his body partially blocked her from skirting around him. "*Nice* is too bland a word for a woman with a vocabulary like yours," he murmured. Their bodies brushed and he felt her inhale with a shiver. Oh, the attraction was still there. Still simmering.

"If I tell you what I thought, we won't leave my hotel room. And as good as that sounds, I'm actually very hungry."

He stepped aside as he laughed. "That I'll believe. It's been a long time since lunch."

Molly looked a little surprised at how he moved aside, so he gave a shrug. "There's no rush. We have all night. If we want it."

She didn't answer. But that was fine, too. When the time came, he'd be sure they were both on the same page. Eyes wide open.

The dining room was about two-thirds full, but the host led them to a table for two, seated next to a wall of windows that overlooked the forest. Twilight was setting in, so that the trees looked more like forms and shadows than branches and leaves, but that was just fine. His attention, for once, wasn't going to be on the view.

They ordered starters of crab cakes and a glass of white wine, and he let her guide the conversation around their trip thus far, an easy and enjoyable topic. While Molly ordered planked halibut for her entrée, Eric decided on a small striploin and added king crab legs to it, and then they tried new wines to pair with each dish. They lingered long into the evening, sharing long glances and smiles, moving on to talking about their jobs and their lives.

The more Molly talked, the livelier her eyes became, sparkling and teasing. He picked at his potato, wondering why he couldn't have met her years ago. Even though he shouldn't have, he found himself comparing her to Murielle and realized that Murielle had that cool reserve thing going on but Molly…she was warm and vibrant.

"You've gone quiet," she said, leaning over and touching his hand. She left her fingers on his skin and he turned his hand over and clasped hers.

"Sorry. Just thinking."

"About?"

"How I wish I'd met you ten years ago."

Her eyes widened but she smiled. "Don't say things like that, Eric. Remember, we only have a few days together. Then we have to go back. We have jobs. Responsibilities."

"I know."

And he did know. He ran a multibillion-dollar corporation. He didn't have the luxury of taking a flight of fancy. Just a small detour.

"I'm glad we met," she continued, squeezing his fingers. She looked down, then met his gaze again. "To be honest, I was starting to wonder if I had this in me."

"Had what?" He frowned, not quite understanding.

"This sense of adventure. Of…fun. My life back home…it's different. That night at the auction? That's my typical evening out. A fund-raiser. A dinner with the right people, or perhaps catching up with some college friends who want to share success stories. It's not exactly…real. Some of our clients are very high-profile." She tapped the side of her nose and said, "Like a certain actor who has a summer home on the Cape where he lives with his ex's best friend."

He remembered the story. Not that he paid much attention to tabloids, but it had been everywhere. You had to live under a rock to not know who she was talking about.

It also meant that such high-profile clients meant high-profile fees. She'd bid over twenty thousand dollars on this trip. He knew because she'd outbid him by a mere hundred dollars. She certainly didn't need a man to make her feel secure or to provide for her. Molly had accomplished that all on her own.

It was kind of refreshing, actually. Because he knew she wasn't hanging on to him because of his money. In the months since the divorce, he'd approached every date with a sense of cynicism in that regard. But not with Molly.

"So you're really getting out?"

She nodded. "Yeah. I'm not sure how yet. I mean, I could take time off and be fine, of course. But I need a purpose. I'd like to find that first before I pull the plug."

"Makes sense."

"What about you?"

He gave his head a small shake. "What about me?"

"Will life be the same for you when you go back?"

No, he wanted to answer, but he held back. The truth was, he wasn't satisfied with his life, either, but had no idea what he'd change. There'd be no Molly. The thought dampened his mood, like snuffing out a candle. One thing he'd definitely like to do, though, was reconnect with his family more, so he said so.

"I'd like to hang out with my brothers again. See if we can't fix what went wrong. And my mother, too." He sighed. "Looking back, I might have contributed more to the problem than I thought. I kept telling myself that my family thought I was too good for them. But maybe—maybe I thought it, too."

"Oh, Eric. I'm sorry. It's not too late, though."

"I hope not. I mean, when my dad left, it fell to me to kind of hold things together, you know? I was the oldest. For me it was all about having enough food on the table. Clothes for the boys for school. Making sure the heat wasn't turned off in the winter."

That was how he'd defined caring for someone. But what if that wasn't what they wanted? Had they wanted more of him and less of his money?

"It's a lot for a young boy to take on. I'm sure they know how hard you worked and appreciate it."

But he wasn't sure they did, so he turned the spotlight back on her.

"What about your family? How do you think they'll take you leaving the firm?"

She shrugged, but her eyes grew troubled. "I don't know. I want to believe they'll want me to be happy. That they won't see it as a betrayal. I know they love me. I think they've just never seen me for me, and like you, I'm partly to blame. I went along with what they wanted because I didn't want to rock the boat. I was the child that lived, you see." She took a drink of wine, put down her glass. "I can stand up to anyone in my job. But it's different when it's your daddy."

He wouldn't know, but he knew what she meant.

"Now," he said, brightening his voice, "let's leave the heavy topics behind for a better one. What's for dessert?"

"Oh, after that meal, I really shouldn't."

"Why not?"

"Oh, you know the old saying. 'A moment on the lips, forever on the hips.'" She rolled her eyes a bit, but he pinned her with his gaze.

"Molly Quinn. There is nothing wrong with your hips. Or any other part of your body, either. Trust me."

She looked up, met his gaze and said blankly, "You're only saying that because I'm wearing Spanx under my dress."

"I am not. I'm pretty sure you weren't wearing that when we were kayaking, or snorkeling, and let me tell you, I couldn't take my eyes off you."

She paused, and seemed to go back and forth in her mind for a minute. And then she said, "Screw it. Let's have dessert."

He handed her the menu with a silent promise to himself that if he had the chance, tonight they'd work off any dessert calories and more.

Damn, he was going to miss her when this was over.

Molly savored every bite of dinner, and when her white-chocolate crème brûlée came, she was determined to enjoy it, too. She ordered a glass of ice wine to go with it, while Eric ordered a cognac and also some sort of flourless chocolate torte that looked divine.

"You can taste mine if I can taste yours," he said, peering around the candles at her ramekin. "That looks incredible."

Indeed it did. White-chocolate shavings sat prettily atop the torched crust of the dessert, along with a bright, fat raspberry. "Deal. But I get to break the crust."

He grinned. "Of course."

She pierced it with her spoon and scooped up the first bite. Taste exploded in her mouth—rich creamy custard and the white chocolate that somehow had a hint of vanilla in it. "Oh, my God. Go ahead. It's incredible."

He took a spoonful and she watched as he put the utensil to his lips. Lord, he was pretty. Maybe she should think handsome, but his face was so perfect, his eyes so heavily lashed. More than once tonight she'd seen him catch the attention of single women in the room. And yet he seemed completely unaware.

She was still trying to digest what he'd told her about his family tonight. To go from worrying about having enough to eat to being a billionaire—what a transformation. It took a strong, determined man to achieve what he had.

When he'd tasted, he offered her his plate. "Try it. It looks decadent."

It was. The complete opposite from her white chocolate and custard, the torte was dense and dark and sinfully delicious.

"This was such a good idea," she said and sighed.

"I don't know why you think you shouldn't eat dessert. There's nothing wrong with your figure."

"Well, I'm not a size six like my mom. She's worked diligently to keep it that way since college."

"So what?" Eric took a bite of his torte, and also took a moment to enjoy it. When he opened his eyes he smiled at her. "Who needs you to be a size six? Who needs you to be anything other than who you are?"

She sat back. "You have to understand. Hearing you say that sounds so…foreign. Particularly when who I am is rarely good enough, or hinges on…"

She stopped, then met his gaze. "Hinges on me doing what my family thinks is right for me."

"I can't understand how this happened. You just don't seem like the type, you know?"

"I know. I truly think it goes back to my brother. I felt the weight of all that expectation. It made me feel responsible. As if maybe, if I could fulfill the dreams they had for him, it would somehow take away the pain of his death." She deliberated for a moment, then confessed, "He was the one who saved me in the water that day. Two months later, he was gone. He saved my life only to lose his. Tell me that isn't cruel and unfair."

He didn't say anything. He didn't have to. She knew how it sounded.

She defiantly ate another bite of dessert, and then Eric said quietly, "So you have a good case of survivor's guilt. But you can't always live your life for him, Molly."

"I know. And my parents are good people. Privileged, yeah. But when he died, I remember the horrible weight of grief around the house. How my mom hugged me a little too tight at night, and Dad walked around looking as if he'd been kicked. I tried to make it better however I could. To make it up to them somehow." She was abashed to find tears on her lashes. She dotted them away with her napkin and took a steadying breath.

"Then maybe they'll be proud of you for being you, too."

"Maybe. I think, though, they'll see it as a betrayal. And I'm not sure how to get around that. I'd like their support."

"You'll have it."

"How do you know?"

He leaned forward. "Because anyone who really knows you can't resist you."

Heat rushed up her cheeks. "Oh, go on."

He laughed. "I said it and I meant it."

They finished their dessert and then it was time for the bill. Eric signed off on it, reminding her that he'd been the one to ask her to dinner, and then put his hand solicitously along her back as they left the dining room. She leaned into the feeling of his warm palm, protective and only a little bit possessive, not shying away from the fact that they were together. And then they ambled back to the guest rooms.

"I have a bottle of red in the room. Care for a nightcap?" he asked.

They both knew he was asking her to his room for more than a glass of wine, and Molly considered the clothes she was wearing. She still wasn't confident, but if Eric were going to see her undressed tonight, she didn't want his first image to be that of her supportive undergarment that "smoothed out her lumps."

"I have one in my room as well," she replied. "Compliments of the tour company. There's no way I can drink it all myself."

He tugged on her hand and she turned around so they were facing. He leaned in and put his lips to hers, the touch warm and firm and surprisingly gentle.

"What was that for?" she asked, when he'd pulled away.

"Something to keep me going until we get there." He kissed her again, until her knees felt like jelly and she found herself melting into his arms. If he kissed her like that again, they'd never make it back to her room.

Somehow they did, and she got out her key with trembling fingers. With one foot in front of the other she made it inside the room, while he shut the door with a firm click behind her.

Wine. Wine would buy her some time to get herself together.

She went to the table and opened the bottle, putting it down to let it breathe a bit. Eric stood in the middle of the room, in his jeans and shirt, looking good enough to eat. Her throat tightened. Where had all this nervousness come from? It wasn't like this was her first time, after all. And yet the way his dark eyes settled upon her had her unnerved.

"Moll," he said softly, and she crossed to him, slipping into his arms as he kissed her fully this time, a bit wildly, and very differently from any of the times before. This kiss was openmouthed and hot, with very little in

the way of restraint. Her body shook as she kissed him back, then moved away when he reached for the tie on the side of her dress.

"Wait a minute," she said, more breathless than she cared to admit. She stepped back and put her hands to her cheeks. "Just…give me a few minutes. Why d-don't you—you p-pour the wine, okay?" She was stammering but couldn't seem to stop, even when she took a reassuring breath. "O-okay. I'll be back in a few minutes." And with that she darted away, grabbing a slip of silk from a drawer as she rushed to the bathroom.

Inside, she braced her hands on the edge of the sink while she tried to control her breathing. A glance in the mirror showed bright eyes and dots of color in her cheeks, as well as a few strands of hair loosened from he messy topknot. She left her hair as it wa then pressed a cool washcloth to her chee This was it. When she went back out th they were going to go to bed together was going to see her…but she remem how he said he liked curves and she to God he wasn't lying. With trembl gers she untied the bow at her wais dress gaped open. Beneath it was shaper, and she peeled it off, then herself in the mirror. She had

what? And a little paunch, but then, who didn't? Why did she need to be perfect?

She left her panties on and then shimmied into the nightgown she'd snagged from her drawer, a peach silk-and-lace one that was held up by spaghetti straps and fell to just above her knee—it was pretty and feminine and made her feel indulgent. For once she was grateful for her love of expensive underwear. It wasn't the raciest outfit, but it wasn't exactly her grandmother's flannel nightie, either.

She could do this. She wanted to do this.

And so, with one last deep breath, she opened the bathroom door and stepped out. Eric was waiting with two glasses of wine in his hands, and his eyes widened when he saw her.

"Goddamn," he breathed, stepping forward. "You're beautiful, Molly. Maybe the most beautiful woman I've ever seen."

He handed her a glass of wine, and for once, she truly believed him.

CHAPTER NINE

MOLLY ROLLED OVER and discovered Eric still sleeping; he'd stayed the night, despite how they'd talked about him going back to his room before morning in an effort to keep things private within the group. But then they'd been talking while basking in some serious afterglow and must have drifted off. He was facing her right now, his long lashes resting on his cheeks, the night's stubble darkening his jaw and the lines around his eyes relaxed. She slowly stretched, feeling delightfully limber. Last night's massage, bath, wine and after-hours activity had made her muscles very, very happy.

She smiled and let out a sigh. Not just her muscles. *She* was happy, too. This living-in-the-moment thing was darn nice. She knew it couldn't last forever, and a slight sense of unease slid through her as she realized that soon they would have to say goodbye.

It wouldn't be as easy as going their separate ways with a wave and a smile. At least it wouldn't be for her. She didn't just fall into bed with anyone, and Eric was not truly the boorish grump who'd walked into her hotel room on day one. He was caring and patient and fun. He'd held her hand during her panic attack, talked her into smashing her phone and sat with her in the night when she had nightmares. An ordinary, selfish guy didn't do those things.

He'd described himself as a workaholic, but she hadn't seen that part of him at all. And he'd admitted that he hadn't paid enough attention to his marriage. She liked him a lot, and it was hard to reconcile the man she was coming to know with the man who lived for work and was emotionally unavailable. His words, not hers.

Maybe this wasn't the real him. Or maybe it was…

He snuffled and shifted beneath the sheets, and she frowned. He could probably say the same about her. She was usually far more self-assured and confident, but the last few days in particular she'd allowed herself to be vulnerable. Which person was the real her? Which did she want to be?

His lashes fluttered open and he gave her a soft and sexy smile. "Good morning."

His deep voice slid over her nerve endings like chocolate, rich and decadent. He reached out and snagged her by the waist, dragging her closer. Then he dipped his head into the curve of her neck and kissed it softly.

He was such a good lover. Her heart stuttered. And a friend, too. How unusual to find both in the same person.

"You should probably get back to your room. It's nearly seven."

He nodded. "I know. There's hanging out together and then there's staying in each other's rooms. I understand not wanting to inspire that kind of chatter in the group."

She relaxed in relief, but he added, "Not that it's anyone's business. We're adults and we're not with anyone else." A startled look came over his face. "At least I'm not. Are you?"

She shook her head wildly. "No, of course not! I would never—"

"I didn't think you would. But I wanted to make sure."

They really didn't know that much about each other. The fact that she wanted to know everything scared her to death. This couldn't go on past their trip, and now she was getting in too deep.

He reached out and tipped up her chin with a finger. "Hey. You're not having second thoughts, are you?"

Was she? No. She was just having other thoughts that were unsettling, to put it mildly. "No, of course not," she answered, pasting on a smile. "Last night was…amazing. I'm just trying to regain my balance. This is kind of unlike me, you know?"

"And you have some things to sort through." He nodded as if he understood, confusing her even more. Was he really as good as he seemed?

"I do."

"Well, if it helps, this isn't my usual speed, either." He let his finger trace along her jaw. "I mean, I'd been with Murielle for a long time. I never cheated, and since the split, I haven't… Well." His full lips twitched a little and his eyes twinkled. "You're my first fling."

It was flattering and frustrating all at the same time. She hated the word *first*. It presumed there would be others after her, and she didn't like that picture in her head.

Then there was the term *fling*. It was very clear that this was a short-term, vacation-only affair. It couldn't be anything else. So why did it bug her so much to be a *first fling*?

She rolled over to her back and kept the covers pulled up under her armpits, even though her peach nightie was back on. "We really should get up. Today we have the morning hike and then on to Tofino. I don't want to keep the group waiting."

His eyes darkened. "Well, you're probably right. I should go shower and pack." He leaned over and dropped a kiss on her nose. "But will you meet me for breakfast?"

She nodded. "Sure. In an hour?"

"Sounds good."

Then there was the moment when he crawled out of bed and she got a tempting glimpse of the rear view as he stood to slip into his shorts and then jeans. He left his shirt untucked, just like last night, only now it was a mess of wrinkles from being on her floor.

She seriously couldn't be sorry. She liked him so much. If circumstances were different, she might even find herself falling for him.

But, circumstances being what they were, that was out of the question.

"I'll see you soon," she said quietly.

He came over to the side of the bed and sat down. "You're sure you're okay?"

She nodded, because she was, even if her mind was going a mile a minute. "I promise I'm fine. More than fine." That was true, too. It was being more than fine that had her tied up in knots.

He leaned over again and touched his lips to hers. "Thanks for the slumber party," he said, then winked at her. She couldn't help the bubble of laughter that rose in her chest at his impish expression.

"Next time we'll braid each other's hair."

"So there'll be a next time?" His voice was so hopeful that she knew last night was not "it." There were four days left of this trip and four days they could enjoy each other. How could she say no when she didn't really want to?

"No promises," she said softly. "But this doesn't feel over yet, does it?"

He jumped up and grinned. "So. Breakfast. One hour. And then it's off to hike in the rain forest."

When he was gone, Molly stretched in the bed and sighed. This was too amazing to be real, wasn't it? At some point, there was going to be a thud, because there always was. She'd been here before. Oh, not with the fling but with relationships. There was a period of time where it was magical and then reality stepped in. Thud. Next thing you knew, it was all over. She'd seen it too many times—in her own life, and every day in her career.

She got out of the bed and hit the shower, then dressed in skinny jeans, sneakers and a T-shirt. Walking through the forest didn't require her to dress up, and she put her hair in a perky ponytail and put some lip gloss on her lips in lieu of full makeup.

Breakfast was coffee and pastries filled with fresh blueberries and white chocolate; not exactly healthy but incredibly delicious. They sat together in the van, then hiked through the incredible Cathedral Grove old forest, with trees so tall it seemed they touched the sky. The guide took a photo of four of them "hugging" one tree just off the trail, and even then their fingers barely touched as they tried to reach around the circumference.

Thanks to the late night and the morning hike in the fresh air, Molly fell asleep in the van during the afternoon drive, which took them to the west coast of the island and the town of Tofino. The resort was small but lovely, with a day spa that catered to the whims of the guests. Molly went ahead with a facial and a pedicure, followed by a heavenly hot-stone massage. Anticipation curled low in her belly when she thought of the night ahead. Would they go back to her room after dinner, or perhaps stop in his?

Later, she stood in front of the full-length mirror in her room and looked herself over with a critical eye.

The silky panties and bra still fit the same, but she felt stronger and leaner, either from the physical demands of the trip or perhaps, she thought, some renewed confidence in herself. She turned sideways and squinted at the little belly just below her navel. It seemed...normal. Not perfect, but why did it have to be perfect? Why did she? She ran her fingers over the skin there and shivered, remembering Eric's hands last night. He hadn't complained about her figure. Her face heated. Nope. He'd done just the opposite.

She went to the closet and took out her best little black dress and highest heels. The dress was a silky, stretchy number that plunged down to just above the middle of her bra and stopped about three inches shy of her knees. Modest enough to be appropriate, but also sexy as hell. She pulled it on without her body shaper underneath and slipped on her heels. She dug out her curling iron and added some loose curls, then shook them out with her fingers and left her hair down. Her eyes, carefully shadowed and mascaraed, glowed back at her in the bathroom mirror. This was a different Molly. A freer one, on her own terms.

It was a woman she liked a lot. Smart. Sexy. Not afraid to take a few chances.

And right now, that chance was probably sitting downstairs at the bar, waiting for a dinner companion.

She grabbed her small purse and pressed her hand one last time to her belly, then let out the breath she'd been holding. It was now or never.

Dinner tonight was different. There was no will-they-or-won't-they? vibe, or any careful conversation to lead up to that do-you-want-to-come-in-for-a-drink? moment. Instead, Eric gave her a once-over when she approached the bar, his dark eyes lit with approval. "I'm going to like taking that off you later," he murmured as he kissed her cheek.

She grinned and whispered back, "I'm not wearing any Spanx."

He laughed as he took her hand and led her to their table. "Oh, dear. What would your mother say?"

"Oh, nothing. I'd just get the *look*."

"What look?"

She did her best impression and he chuckled again. "Ah, I see. The look that says, 'Darling, really? Are you sure that's your best look?'"

This time she laughed out loud. "Oh, you nailed it. Anyway, tonight I decided it was time for me to be, well, me for a change."

"Again, good choice." They ordered wine, and when it arrived, Eric lifted his glass and they touched rims before drinking. The waiter came by to take their orders, and after he was gone, Eric caught her hand in his and rubbed his thumb over the soft skin at the base of her thumb. "You know, back there I thought you were going to say you weren't wearing any underwear." His eyes twinkled devilishly. "Instead you're just not…"

"Strapped in?" she suggested, and then turned his hand over and rubbed along the same spot with her thumb. "Well, to be honest, I am wearing underwear, but not much."

His throat bobbed as he swallowed.

"You started it," she said, biting down on her lip.

He stopped the motion of her thumb by twining his fingers with hers. "How about tonight we skip dessert?" he asked.

* * *

Eric took several deep breaths, willing his heart rate to lower. If kayaking had been Molly's big challenge during the trip, today was his. Zip-lining in the rain forest outside Ucluelet. Heights were just not his thing. Particularly heights when one was hanging from some questionable-looking hooks and ropes.

"Hi," she said, bouncing up beside him. "How'd you sleep?"

His nervousness was temporarily forgotten at her cheeky question. "Like a babe," he replied, looking over at her. "All that fresh air yesterday, I guess."

"Me too." Her lips twitched, and with total disregard for the fact they were in public, he grabbed her around the waist and pulled her in for a kiss. When he released her she was speechless.

"That's for being saucy."

Her eyes were starry and her lips puffy, but her tongue was just as sharp as ever. "Then I'll be sure to be saucy more often."

He laughed. She had this uncanny way of making him do that. Forget all the things swirling around his brain and just have fun. If he didn't know better, he'd say he loved her for it.

Of course, that was a ridiculous notion. Love wasn't part of the equation. Fun was.

Except they were in these strange harnesses and preparing to step off a perfectly good platform into nothingness. Not that he'd let on that he was scared. No way. He set his teeth. He could charm. He could be honest. But he could never, ever let himself show actual weakness. He hadn't gained his success by letting himself be visibly vulnerable. He was rather good at bluffing, though.

The team waiting for them was made up of college-age guys with hair a little on the long side, big laughs, and they said "dude" a lot. They were also incredibly efficient and firm when it came to safety, which Eric appreciated. Still, as they neared the first platform, sweat broke out on his back. He adjusted the helmet on his head and wiped his hands on his shorts.

One of the team leaders zipped off first, the line singing as gravity pulled him away, and he would be waiting at the platform at the other end for the first of their group.

Eric knew he shouldn't go last, but he couldn't seem to make himself get in line earlier. Molly was two people ahead of him, and she turned around with a bright smile. He smiled back and waved, but an odd look came over her face. A few seconds later she stepped out of line and came back to him.

"What's the matter? Don't you feel good? You've gone white."

She'd just given him the out he'd needed. "I don't know. Breakfast isn't settling too well. Maybe it was the smoked salmon."

She frowned. "I had the same and I feel okay." Another of their group took off with a joyful whoop. "Do you want to stay behind? I'll stay with you if you're sick."

He could say yes, but he wasn't used to chickening out. Besides, she'd be giving up on part of her adventure, and she'd gone kayaking even though she'd been terrified. If she could, he could. "I'll be fine."

The guy from Arizona was next, all six foot five of him, and off he went through the trees and across the tumbling stones of the riverbed.

That left the two of them and the final guide.

"You go," she said, "and I'll come right behind you. Okay?"

"Okay."

But he stood up to the edge, and as the guide clipped him onto the line, he couldn't make his feet move.

"You nervous, dude? It's okay. Lots of people are."

Eric looked at the guy, who was maybe twenty-two. He expected to see some arrogance or ridicule, but what he got in return was understanding and patience. "I don't do heights."

"It's a common thing. It's okay. Take your time. Then you just have to step off the platform. You don't have to leap or anything."

"Step off the platform—easy for you to say."

Molly showed up by his side. "Are you afraid of heights?"

He laughed. "Of course not." At her skeptical expression, he sighed. "I'm terrified. I can't actually make my feet move right now."

"You don't have to do this," she said quietly, "but I know you can."

"Like you did the morning after you capsized."

"You were with me. These cables can handle a lot more than your weight, okay? Just let it take your weight and gravity will do the rest. And I'll see you in a few minutes. Can you step to the edge?"

He made his feet move, finally. He went to the edge of the wood platform and looked down. It wasn't far, but it was far enough.

"Do you ski? This is no higher than a ski lift. And those are run by cables, too."

"I hate the ski lift," he growled, and Molly burst out laughing.

"Of course you do."

He could do this. There wasn't much in life that he found daunting, but heights made him feel light in the stomach and weak in the knees. He'd conquered so much; surely he could do this, too.

He'd known all along this part of the trip would happen. He'd psyched himself up for it, and now he was psyching himself out. Well, no more. He sent Molly a grin and then, with his heart in his throat, stepped off the edge.

The first sensation was that of the cable taking his weight and then bouncing back up a bit. Then it was the sound, the whirring *zing* of the wire as he zipped through the forest and out to the riverbed. He kept both hands on the ropes in front of him that connected him from harness to cable, and before he knew it, he'd arrived at the platform and the other guide was unclipping him to prepare for Molly's arrival.

He'd done it! And it hadn't been scary, not after that first moment. It had been exhilarating!

A distant humming sound touched his ears and he looked up to see the cable bouncing a bit and Molly's form getting closer. The brake mechanism caught her just before the platform and she laughed, grinning from ear to ear as she was unhooked and set free. "So?" she asked, rushing forward to grab his hand. "You made it!"

"I did. And I didn't even pass out. Not once I stepped off into nothing."

"Probably because at that point there was no turning back."

"You're not wrong." He chuckled and they watched as their guide zipped in and the group then got ready for the next zip line.

The various lines took them over the Kennedy River Canyon; over craggy rocks and rushing water, even under a bridge. The more Eric did, the more he enjoyed it and let go of the death grip on the ropes in front of him. He laughed out loud when Molly came rushing over the canyon in a starfish pose. God, she was so beautiful when she was free and open like this. The same way she was in bed, he realized. She stopped overthinking and just was, and so did he. They were good for each other.

To his surprise, he really didn't want this trip to end. He couldn't imagine flying away and never seeing her again. But he also couldn't think how they might make something work between them. They didn't even live in the same country.

He looked over at her, talking to the same Alberta couple that she'd made friends with earlier in the trip. Her arms were moving as she told some sort of story, her face alight with fun and happiness. He needed that in his life, desperately. He knew how to make money, but he didn't know how to be happy. He hadn't focused on simple joy since he was twelve and his life had changed overnight. But that had changed this week, with Molly, and he didn't want it to end.

The final zip of the day was next and no one could be more surprised than him that he wished it wasn't over. One final rush and his feet were on solid ground again. He removed his helmet and harness and swiped a hand through his sweaty hair. The first thing he wanted to do back at the resort was have a shower, or maybe go for a swim in the Pacific. For all their snorkeling and kayaking, they had yet to have an actual ocean swim.

They were on their way back to the resort when he suggested it, pleased when Molly readily agreed despite her hesitation about the water. They made plans to grab a light picnic supper and head to the sand before their departure back to Victoria tomorrow.

Molly wore the simple one-piece suit she'd worn in the hot tub back in Campbell River, with a sheer cover-up over the top and flip-flops on her feet. The beach was a short walk from the resort, and he carried the picnic basket while she managed a beach bag with towels and a blanket for sitting on. It was late afternoon by the time they reached the long stretch of white sand, and Eric took a deep breath of sea air. They walked down the beach far enough that there was no one around, and Molly spread out the blanket.

He reached for her and pulled her in for a kiss. "Know what? This makes me wish it were just you and me on a desert island somewhere. We could swim naked and eat coconuts all day."

Her hands slid up his back. "What about fresh water? And a diet of only coconuts would probably cause us some gastro distress."

"You're no fun."

"I'm very fun. And I don't want to be anywhere other than where I am right now."

"I second that," he said and kissed her again, long and deep, until she made a little sighing sound in the back of her throat.

He pulled away and put his hand on her face. "This is getting complicated, isn't it?"

"I want to say no, but…"

"I know. I like you more than I wanted to, Molly. It's not just about this attraction thing. Today I did something that scared me to death and I was willing to let you see it. And you helped me, you know? I don't usually let myself be vulnerable."

Her gaze softened. "You trusted me."

"It's not a very common phenomenon with me. I don't trust people."

"Because the one person you were supposed to be able to trust let you down?"

He nodded. "Yeah. Why is it stuff that happened when we were kids seems to leave such an indelible mark?"

"I don't know. Maybe because when we're kids, we don't have the experience or maturity to deal with it, and we just carry it with us to deal with later."

"Well, it sucks."

She reached for his hand and laughed a little. "It definitely does, but we can talk about it later. Let's make like seals and go play in the water."

He couldn't resist her. With each day that passed, she seemed to let her hair down a little more. And so did he, metaphorically speaking. He peeled off his T-shirt and followed her into the water, where heavy breakers sent froth over the sand. "Be careful!" he called out.

"Don't worry!" she shouted back, turning around. "I've come a long way this week, but not that far."

So she still had some fear about the water then. He let the waves buffet him as he waded out to where she was and took her hand. "You know how to swim, though?"

She nodded. "Yeah. I just haven't in a really long time."

"You could float on the waves. I'll hold your hand."

"And you'll pull me up if I get swamped by a wave?"

"I promise."

She looked up at him, her hair blowing around her face. "I trust you, Eric."

And with those words, he felt himself fall for her. All the way.

Damn.

CHAPTER TEN

MOLLY EASED HERSELF into the water and then let her feet leave the bottom so that she was floating on the waves. They were out far enough that her body rose and fell with the swell but didn't get caught in the breakers, and Eric held her hand—he was her lifeline. She did trust him. In fact, she was pretty sure she was falling in love with him. This afternoon had sealed it. He'd seemed too in control and competent during the whole trip, but today he'd been afraid and he'd let her see it. For the first time in her life, she felt as if she were involved with an equal. Someone who knew some of her deepest vulnerabilities and didn't judge her for them, and who offered the same in return. They'd said they were going to take things day by day, but the trip was nearing its end. Tomorrow was back to Victoria, and then a final free day in the city to sightsee as they pleased. How could she say goodbye with a smile on her face, when her heart was sure to be hurting?

She was floating on the ocean with the sexiest, strongest man she'd ever met acting as her anchor.

As she floated, she thought back to her life in Boston, and the charity event that had brought her to this place, and wondered if she could do something in the nonprofit field. Would that be more fulfilling? For starters, she could offer some services pro bono for the opioid clinic. And then look for a position where she'd truly be of use.

A sense of peace and rightness flowed over her, and she let go of Eric's hand and flipped over so she was bobbing in the water. His face was blank with surprise, so she grinned and did something she wouldn't have been able to imagine even two weeks ago: she ducked under the water and swam with strong strokes out into the waves. When she surfaced, she let them carry her back in, where he caught her in his arms. Instead of letting her feet touch the ground, she wrapped her legs around his waist and put her arms around his neck.

"You amaze me," he said, leaning back to look her square in the face.

"I've amazed myself. And it's because of

you, Eric. I couldn't have done any of this without you."

The only problem was figuring out how to say goodbye, because while she'd finally had a kernel of an idea about her professional life, she couldn't seem to figure out a way for them to work out, and the clock was ticking down.

The city of Victoria was stunning in its own right, situated on the southern tip of Vancouver Island. The tour group was ending, with one last luncheon together before everyone went their separate ways for a self-guided twenty-four hours of sightseeing. Molly and Eric sat together as the group ate a delicious lunch with a view of the harbor, and then said heartfelt goodbyes to their travel mates and guides. She could hardly believe it was all coming to an end.

After lunch, she popped into a store and bought a cheap pay-as-you-go phone. In a few days she'd be back home, and she was hoping one of her parents could pick her up from the airport. She needed to see them. Needed to be home, in the house where she'd grown up, and get her bearings before broaching the topic of her leaving the firm. She had to make her parents understand that leaving the firm didn't mean leaving them. They hadn't been perfect but they'd been good parents. Losing a child had left its mark, but there was no doubt in Molly's mind that they'd loved her and had mourned Jack terribly.

She was holding on to the idea of that love carrying them through what she was sure was going to be a disappointment.

Molly and Eric had planned a late-afternoon trip to Butchart Gardens, so in the meantime she popped up to her room to freshen up and to make a call. Her first one was to Ryan, where she left a voice mail asking him about the opioid center and if he had some contacts there she could speak with. Then she called her mom, who let out a huge sigh of relief at hearing Molly's voice and immediately agreed to meet her at the airport after her flight.

She was going home. Leaving tomorrow night and taking the red-eye.

Away from Eric.

Tears stung the backs of her eyes and she sniffled, allowing herself the moment of sadness in the privacy of her hotel room. He was a once-in-a-lifetime guy and it sucked that she had to leave him behind. There was no other way to look at it.

When it was time to meet him downstairs, she dropped her phone into her bag and touched up her makeup; she didn't want him to see that she'd been crying. Ryan hadn't called back, so she locked the door behind her and figured future plans could wait. Right now she wanted to spend every last moment she could with Eric.

He was waiting for her at the doors, and her heart leaped at the sight of him. His smile was just for her, and he kissed her cheek and told her he'd hired a car to take them to the gardens and back.

The car wasn't just a car—it was a limousine, and Molly felt slightly conspicuous and very pampered. Once at the gardens, Eric paid their admission and they meandered through the various styles of garden. The Japanese garden was tranquil and serene, with flowing water, Japanese maples, and rhododendrons everywhere. The rose garden was nothing short of absolute splendor, boasting over two hundred varieties of roses and a trellised archway heavy with climbing blooms. The scent was heavenly, and Molly gave a happy sigh at the sensory delight it provided. Eric bought them gelato at the Italian Garden, the sweet and cool treat a perfect choice for the heat of the late afternoon. Molly's favorite, though, was the Sunken Garden. The paths led around it but the colors were bright and showy and simply stunning. They found a vacant bench and sat for a few minutes, eating their cones of gelato, enjoying the sun.

"I'm going to miss you," Eric said, his voice low.

The words sent a pang through her heart and she lowered her cone. "Oh, Eric, me too. This has been so incredible. I can't believe it's over tomorrow...but it is. We can't freeze time."

"Would you? If you could?"

A lump formed in her throat. "I would. Even though it would hurt more to leave you the longer we're together. I just... I don't know. We haven't talked about what's next. I don't think we've wanted to, and spoil the moment."

"My business is headquartered out of Montreal."

"And I'm not licensed to practice in Canada."

"And it would be silly to talk about things like...relocating based on a vacation fling."

She met his gaze. "This wasn't just a fling for me. Just so you know."

"For me, either."

Her heart stuttered. They were laying it all out there now. They genuinely cared for each other. It was in all they said and didn't say. She got up and took her half-eaten gelato to a trash can; she was no longer hungry. When she came back she sat down and took his hands in hers.

"We could try the long-distance thing, maybe. Boston and Montreal aren't that far of a plane ride. Plus you've had business in Boston before…"

His dark eyes plumbed hers. "Could we? Or would it just make things harder?"

Her chest cramped. "I'm just saying…we could try, if we both wanted to. See how it goes."

Tourists milled about, but Molly ignored them as she looked into Eric's face. "I've never felt like this before. I think I want the chance to see what we look like in the real world before I give up."

Eric put his palm against her cheek. "You are the most amazing woman. I arrived here tired and jaded, and now… I can't even describe it. You're different from anyone I've ever met. I can't say no to that."

Relief washed over her and she slid closer for a hug. "Oh, God, I'm so glad to hear you say that. We can figure out the particulars later. I'm just glad tomorrow isn't the very last day and I'll never see you again."

"Me too. And we still have tonight."

Hand in hand, they meandered over to the carousel house, listening to the tinny chime of the music as it went around in circles, to the delight of the handful of children still at the gardens even though the day was growing shorter. "Look," she whispered, pointing. "They're all different animals. Oh, I haven't been on one of these since I was a little girl, and I went on with Jack."

"Then we definitely need a ride," Eric decreed, and once again he fished out the money to pay. When the carousel stopped, they got on. She perched on one of the larger horses, a classic, and instead of getting on his own pony, Eric stood beside her, his hand on the pole, his gaze glued to hers. And when they were spinning around and around to the music, he said, "I'm falling in love with you, Molly."

The impact of those words hit her right in the solar plexus, stealing her breath. No one had ever said those words to her before. They'd liked her, cared about her, had fun with her, but no one had ever used the word *love*, not even at the height of her most serious relationship. He'd used every word but, and it had eaten away at her confidence. For a long time she'd wondered if perhaps she wasn't lovable. Or if she didn't deserve it.

But Eric had just said it. And she was glad that it hadn't happened before. Because at this moment it simply felt *right*.

"I'm falling in love with you, too, Eric."

And when he kissed her she wasn't sure if she was dizzy from the ride or the kiss or a combination of both.

CHAPTER ELEVEN

MOLLY HAD BOOKED a surprise for the morning. Eric had been so wonderful, paying for romantic dinners, and last night, at the gardens…it had been the most perfect evening. After the carousel, they'd wandered through the gardens, lit up especially for the evening, making it a magical fairyland. They'd put up the privacy screen and necked in the limousine on the way back to the hotel, and the night afterward…well, the perfect evening had definitely turned into the perfect night. The least she could do was surprise him with something amazing.

He'd gone back to his room for a shower and clean clothes when her phone rang. She rushed to pick it up; only her family and Ryan had her current number.

"Hey, gorgeous. You rang?"

She laughed at the teasing note in his voice. "You got my message about the charity?"

"Sure did, and they'd be glad of the help. I spoke to the executive director this morning. But I have another idea for you. There's a company here that could use some expertise. It's not quite up your alley, but I thought of you because it's something I've been really aware of as a doctor. There's a company here in Massachusetts that's being bought out by some conglomerate. The thing is, they're a leading research and manufacturer of pros-thetics. The R-and-D side is in great shape, but some mismanagement has put them in the red. They're working to fight the bid, but this guy has put forward a compelling offer. I'd hate to see that company bought and sold off piece by piece, you know?"

Hope slammed into her chest. "I know someone with a lot of expertise in this area! Can you email me the details? I'll see what I can do."

"Does this mean you're getting out of the divorce market?"

"Unofficially? Yes. But I haven't talked to my dad yet, so please keep it quiet, okay?"

"Of course. I'm just glad that I had you for my divorce. Once you get something in your teeth, you're like a pit bull. You don't let go."

"I think I'll take that as a compliment?"

"The highest kind. I'll send through that

info right away. Have a look and see what you think. Again, it's not exactly in your wheelhouse, but sometimes an outside perspective is a great thing."

They hung up and Molly sat down on the edge of the bed, wondering what to do with all her energy. First she needed the info from Ryan before she could ask Eric for advice. But she had that elusive purpose now. Something to take her attention while she figured so many other things out. Battling for an underdog sounded perfect.

But now she had to check out of her room. Her heart grew heavy as she packed all her things in her cases. The bathing suit from the hot tub and the beach. Yoga pants and long-sleeved shirts from the kayaking trip. The red dress that had knocked his socks off… and the black one that was her particular favorite. All these clothes now had specific memories associated with them, ones that she'd cherish. But it wouldn't be the same as having Eric with her, making her laugh, taking her breath away.

Before leaving to check out, she glanced at her phone. Ryan had sent her links to articles surrounding the health of the company and the struggles it would face to recover. She spent twenty minutes going over the material—if she talked to Eric, she wanted to at least brush up on the particulars. According to one source, two companies had been interested in taking over Atlantic Bionics. Now it was down to one. He also left a parting note that if she came on board, she'd have access to more detailed material.

Tonight she'd be leaving Eric. The idea that she might have something to go home to was a lifeline she latched on to.

They met in the lobby, both of them leaving their luggage with the concierge before heading to the hotel restaurant for breakfast. It was there, over blissfully strong coffee and eggs Benedict, that Molly told Eric of the morning's plans.

"So, I have a surprise for you. I've booked us on an aerial tour. I took a chance that your fear of heights doesn't extend to flying, since you travel so much."

"You did?"

She nodded. "An hour above the island, looking at the coast the way the eagles do." She reached over and took his hand. "You'll come?"

"Of course I will. I just wish…"

He hesitated and she met his gaze. "You wish what?"

"I wish we hadn't had to check out. These

are our last hours together. At least…for a while."

She thought of Ryan's phone call and smiled a little. "I might have an idea about that, but it'll keep. Meanwhile, it looks like I'm going to be doing some work for the rehab place, so I've put the wheels in motion. How about you?"

He reached into his pocket and took out a new phone. "I picked up a new one this morning and got about three hundred emails and at least two dozen voice messages. Which is less than I expected, but the moment I get on the plane this afternoon, it's back to the real world."

The thought put a damper on their earlier fun vibe. "This isn't going to be easy, is it?"

He shook his head. "No. So let's enjoy the morning. What time's the flight?"

She grinned, happy again for one last adventure. "In an hour. Let's wander the harbor first, shall we?"

They ambled hand in hand along the streets near the harbor, taking in the shops and late-summer flowers. It really was a pretty city, and it was wonderful to wander on their own, without being part of a bigger group. Their own little trip to enjoy and cherish.

Cherish. That was the second time she'd thought of that word today and it gave her a pang of sadness. It was unfair they had to say goodbye. There were no guarantees it would work out. No matter what happened, after today everything would change. Their little bubble of existence would be popped.

At the appointed time they were at the dock for the floatplane that would take them on their tour. The single-turbine plane had room for six passengers, but it was only the two of them this morning since Molly had booked it as a last-minute private charter.

"Welcome aboard," the pilot greeted them, and with excitement churning through her belly, Molly got in and buckled her seat belt.

"This is pretty cool, Molly." Eric snapped his belt, too, and looked over at her. "I've done a lot of things, but I've never been in a seaplane."

"Me either. I'm a little nervous about the takeoff and landing."

"Don't worry," the pilot called back as the propeller began to spin and the engine revved to life. "Water's nice and smooth today and we have perfect flying conditions. Just sit back and enjoy the flight."

They held hands as the pilot steered the plane out onto the water and then opened up the throttle, propelling them forward and then into the air. The city appeared below them—the stone buildings and vast trees and the white boats bobbing in a perfect rectangle in the inner harbor. They banked to the left, taking them along the southern end of the island, and Molly let out a breath. She peered out the window and took a few pictures with her new phone, and then glanced back at Eric, who should have been watching the scenery but instead had his eyes on her. She'd fallen for him; that was all there was to it.

She was just about to say so when her phone buzzed in her hand. She looked down and saw it was a text from Ryan, and she hurriedly opened the message to see what news he had to her follow-up questions.

You asked about the company with the offer on the table. It's EPC Industries. Owned by a Canadian, Eric Chambault, out of Montreal. Is there more you need?

Molly's gaze snapped over to Eric, who was watching her quizzically. "Is something wrong?" he asked.

"Just some unexpected news." She was still trying to digest it all. "I spoke to Ryan this morning—he's the one I went to the benefit with where I bid on the trip. He's the one who got me the in at the opioid clinic."

"Okay. Go on."

"He's got a personal stake there, so it made sense to call him about it, you know? But this morning he mentioned another project that might need legal help, and he sent a bunch of information through. A business in Waltham, it turns out. Great R-and-D department, doing some really great things. Financially, though, it's been mismanaged, and another company is looking at stepping in and buying them out."

"Huh. Sounds familiar." He smiled at her. "So what's the problem?"

Her stomach turned strangely, and it had nothing to do with the airplane or any turbulence. They weren't even looking at the scenery anymore, and Molly got the feeling she was walking a tightrope, only she wasn't sure why.

"The company is Atlantic Bionics."

His smile dropped. "I see."

"And the company poised to take it over is EPC Industries. You, Eric. Isn't that a crazy coincidence?"

He nodded. "Not so crazy. It's why I was

in Boston last spring, when I saw you at the benefit."

"Well, they want to bring me on board to help fight the takeover." She leaned over and took his hand. "Surely you can see the good of a company like that. Why would you want to strip it and sell the assets? Can't you walk away from this one? Maybe if they're given time, they can come back from their financial issues, you know? I did some quick reading up this morning. They need a guiding hand, not to be torn apart bit by bit."

"I don't 'tear things apart,' Molly. I buy businesses in trouble. Many of them go on in new iterations that are stronger and far more viable."

"But why take over? Why not invest in it instead? Or just leave it alone?"

His mouth dropped open. "Are you seriously asking me to walk away from a multimillion-dollar deal, after we've put countless resources and man-hours into it? As a favor?"

Why was his voice so low and dangerous? Good heavens, for the last week they'd talked lots about making a difference and what didn't make them happy. "Think about it," she continued, injecting some excitement into her voice. "Instead of breaking it up you could help it. Invest in it and make a huge difference! Think of all the people you could help! You said you wanted to get away from everything being about dollar signs—this could be it, Eric."

"So what are you asking? For me to sink money into a dying business, or to walk away from something I've been working on for over a year?"

She sat back. "I—I don't know."

"I didn't think you…" He cursed under his breath, then turned and looked out the window. They were going over some island or something now, but the flight was ruined and she didn't quite know why.

"You're angry."

"I'm angry at myself. For thinking you were different."

The words were like a slap in the face, and Molly retreated as if struck. "What do you mean?" she asked quietly, so quietly her voice could barely be heard over the sound of the engine.

"I never thought you'd trade on my feelings. Use my vulnerabilities against me." His eyes blazed. "I told you before. I might use weaknesses, but I'd never use fears against someone else."

Guilt slammed into her. She had handled

this all wrong. "That wasn't my intention at all. I would never—"

"What's this Ryan's stake, anyway? Why does he care?"

"He's a vascular surgeon. A doctor."

"And how long have you known him?"

"I handled his divorce last winter."

Eric clenched his fingers into fists. Was it possible he'd been played? The deal with Atlantic Bionics had been in development for months, and he'd known there was opposition. The truth was, the manufacturing arm wasn't enough to support the research-and-development side, and as a result both were going to go down. It was no big secret that he was the head of EPC Industries. He didn't want to believe he'd been totally suckered, but he had to ask anyway.

"Was this all part of a master plan, Molly? Because it all seems a little too coincidental to me."

"You think I was a plant?" Her mouth gaped open. "You really think I could…that I would…"

"I don't really know anything about you, do I?" he growled, feeling not only foolish, but also incredibly disappointed. "We've known each other for exactly ten days. Unless, of course, you've done your research."

Her nostrils flared. "You know what? You can say a lot about me but I'm no corporate plant. I had no idea that this was a project of yours or even what your company name was until this morning. Until just now, when he texted. Yeah, it's a hell of a coincidence, but I swear on my brother's grave that I did not come on this trip to... For God's sake. To gain information or try to get you to stop some deal."

"Until now."

"Well, it's important."

Frustration bubbled over. Yes, he believed her. She would never swear on her brother's grave otherwise. Besides, she had a horrible poker face and right now she was angry and hurt at his accusation. There were no tears; that wasn't her style. But her eyes were icy fire as they fell upon him and she did this weird rubbing thing with her lips when she got frustrated. An hour ago they'd been planning one last romantic outing. In the space of three minutes everything seemed to collapse like a house of cards.

"If it's that important," he said, a bit quieter, "then you should go home and do your research. Don't just go by what this Ryan guy tells you. And you're not a corporate lawyer, Molly. You specialize in family law. Let me tell you they're not the same."

"I know how to do research," she snapped.

"Hey, don't get snippy with me. After ten days together, the first thing you do is ask me for a favor. And we're not talking can-you-pick-up-some-antacids-at-the-store kind of favor. You're asking me to throw away a whole business deal because you got a text message that said it should happen. Do you realize how ridiculous that sounds?"

He looked out the window. "Know what bothers me the most? I actually thought you were different. That it wasn't about my money or my status or what I could do for you. Thanks for proving me wrong before I leave tonight. Now I can fly home with a clean conscience."

She faced him then, her eyes wide and hurt. "Know what? Maybe the timing sucks. Maybe the circumstances are messed up. But let's be honest. This is a perfect excuse for you to push me away because you're scared of your feelings. It was fine when we were on the trip, but now that it's time to part and we have to deal with the real world? Yeah. You said yourself you don't do emotional intimacy well, so let's call a spade a spade.

Because I'm coming from a good place here, and you're making me out to be something I'm not."

"Me, scared? That's funny, coming from you."

The look of pain that shot across her face filled him with regret. He should say he was sorry, because he was. She was right. He was afraid. Of his feelings. Of letting old patterns sneak back into his life. She'd opened up a whole new world for him, and instead of thanking her, he was punishing her for it.

She didn't reply, which surprised him, and he didn't look over at her, either. He didn't trust himself to say what was in his heart. The pilot diplomatically flew on as if an argument hadn't just taken place behind him. Eric looked down and saw the city come back into view. In a few minutes they would be landing. He wasn't even going to go back to the hotel with her; he had no idea what he'd say. He was going to head straight to the airport and have his bags delivered to him. The sooner he got home, the better.

This past week he'd been as "emotionally available" as he'd ever been in his life. He didn't let people in. Hell, he hadn't even let

Murielle in, and they'd been married. Now he finally had and look what happened.

What a fool he'd been.

He heard sniffling behind him and closed his eyes. She was crying. He hadn't exactly been gentle with his last words to her, but he was hurt, too, dammit. Last night he'd looked at her and said he was falling in love with her. Now he just felt stupid and raw. He wanted to pull her into his arms and say this had all been a mistake, but something held him back. Maybe she was right. Maybe he was just a coward.

The plane landed with a few bumps on the waves and then a smooth glide into the dock. Molly put her hand on his arm. "Please, can't we talk about this? I know I've messed things up."

He couldn't stand to see her beg. "The last ten days we've ignored reality," he said, looking at her finally, "and now we can't ignore it anymore. This is my life. And that's yours. We were just fooling ourselves. We should just leave it at that." Before he screwed it up worse. And hurt her more than she was already hurting. His gut churned as he realized he'd done that his whole life—he'd driven away his mom, his brothers... Murielle. All because he really had no idea how to love anyone.

Now he cared about her too much to let this go on and make it worse.

"I'm willing to try," she protested, swiping her fingers under her eyes.

He let out a heavy sigh, wanting to give her what she wanted, terribly afraid he'd mess it up just like he'd messed up this morning with his knee-jerk reaction. "We were fooling ourselves into thinking this could somehow work. We had a fling. That's all. Trying to pretend otherwise was bound to fail. This morning just made it clear."

They got out of the plane and he started to walk away, his heart hurting.

Molly reached out and grabbed his arm. "You think this makes it easier?" He heard her sob and closed his eyes again, not wanting to do this on a dock in the middle of the day.

"Don't make it worse than it is," he murmured. "Let me go, Molly. It's for the best."

"You think I used you…well, fine. You go on thinking that, if it makes you sleep better at night. I won't lie to you or to myself. I fell for you and I'm not going to pretend I didn't. And it's not going to be easy to get over you. I shared things I've never shared with anyone else—do you get that? So fine. Let this be your excuse if you want it to be, but let's not lie to ourselves, okay? You—you coward!"

She let go of his arm and rushed by him, her sandals making thudding sounds on the platform. For a moment he considered going after her. But she'd hurt him, too. For a week and a half he'd believed that she had no motives whatsoever. That he could have been an ordinary guy off the street and she would have felt the same, that his money didn't matter.

But maybe there would always be that little bit of doubt. Maybe it was impossible to separate him from the balance sheet, and it would always be this way. It had been for Murielle, who'd hopped on a rising star and demanded his love, but in the end settled for his money. And it had been for each of his dates since the divorce. He'd worked hard for his success, but there was a surprising downside to having the word *billionaire* after your name.

It made trusting impossible. He'd trusted her, though. And that was what hurt the most.

In the end he walked around for a while, then arranged for his bags to be delivered to the airport while he caught a cab. His flight was on time and he stretched out in first class, making the first leg of his trip.

The adventure was over, and it was more bittersweet than he'd ever thought possible.

CHAPTER TWELVE

MOLLY STEPPED INSIDE the brick colonial that had been her childhood home and called out. "Mom? Dad? Are you in?"

Her mother stepped out from the room that had always served as her dad's home office. "We're in here, but just getting ready for a cocktail before dinner. Would you like one?"

God, yes. Tonight's conversation wasn't going to be an easy one and her nerves were jumping all over the place. "A glass of wine, maybe," she replied, thinking it was a better choice than hard liquor. Something to soften the edges of her anxiety, not hit it with a hammer.

She went into the living room while her mother went to get the wine, and wandered around looking at the various pictures on the walls. There was an original from someone her mom liked, and a few prints, but only two framed photos on the top of the piano. One of her on the day she'd graduated from Harvard, and one of her as a little girl, with her brother, Jack, on a first day of school the September before he died. A month after he'd snagged her from the waves and dragged her to safety.

The sign above the office door had two Quinns on it. She was here to tell her dad that it would now be just one. There was no question that he'd be disappointed.

Olivia returned with two glasses of white wine, cold enough that condensation was already starting to bead on the bowls of the glasses. Molly grinned. "You know I like my white very cold," she said and leaned forward to kiss her mom's cheek. "Thank you."

"When you said you wanted to come over and talk to us, you sounded serious. Is everything okay?"

Molly sighed, confusion taking over again. "Yes?"

"*Yes* with a question mark? That doesn't sound too promising."

"I'll wait for Dad to come in. It's something I should talk to you about together."

"All right. So tell me, how was your trip?"

"Amazing. I kayaked with whales and went zip-lining and snorkeled with salmon."

"It sounds very…rustic."

Molly laughed. "It was, and I was out of my comfort zone a lot, but that was kind of the point. I learned a lot about myself, and don't worry—I also made sure to enjoy some great food and wine, spa treatments, and…"

Her voice faltered. She cleared her throat. "And I met some really great people. I give the trip a ten out of ten for sure."

Olivia merely shook her head. "As long as you're happy."

Molly looked into her mother's eyes. "Do you really mean that, Mom?"

"Of course. That's all we've ever wanted for you."

Molly was prevented from asking the natural next question when her dad came in, also holding a glass of wine. "Had to go to the kitchen for my own," he grumbled, but he was smiling. "Hello, pumpkin. Look at you, all tanned from your trip. You survived, I see."

She kissed his cheek. "I did. Even without my phone. And I notice the firm stayed afloat without me, too."

"Barely." But he said it with a smile. "We missed you."

"Dinner will be ready soon. Do you want to go through to the dining room?" her mother asked.

Charles was ready but Molly stopped him with a hand on his arm. "Could we wait a few minutes? I want to talk to you both about something and it might be better done in a room without knives."

"Sounds serious," Charles answered and patted her hand. "Let's sit down, then. Let me guess. You met someone on the trip and you're going to run away." He laughed, clearly joking, but when she didn't laugh back his face fell. "Oh, dear. Did you meet someone and are you going to run away?"

"I'm not running away. Not really," she replied. "And I did meet someone, but it was very clear it was only a vacation romance. So no worries there."

Olivia took the chair to the right of the sofa. "That wouldn't be a worry. It'd be nice to see you in love, honey."

They couldn't know how much those words hurt, so she brushed them off with a small smile. "Believe me, you don't want to hear about my love life. I want to talk to you about my role in the firm. Or rather... Dad, I know you're going to be upset and disappointed, but I want to leave family law. I just... It's soul-sucking."

Charles sat back with a sigh and a look of consternation on his face. "But...it's

Quinn and Quinn. I built this firm for my children…"

"And I'm the only child left. I know that, Dad, and that's what makes this so hard. I know you put all your hopes and dreams on me when Jack died, and I've tried so hard to make you proud. Maybe for both of us."

She'd never said those words aloud before, and Olivia's mouth dropped open. "Oh, Molly. We never intended to make you feel that kind of pressure."

"It's true I always wanted to see another generation on the sign," Charles said and let out a sigh. "But more than that, you're damn good at it, Molly. You always had a ton of potential. If I pushed, it was because I wanted you to realize it."

She uncrossed her legs and leaned her elbows on her knees for a moment. "When Jack died, the house was so quiet. Sometimes I could hear Mom crying. Once I saw you, Dad, sitting at your desk, weeping. I didn't know how else to make it better…"

Her lower lip wobbled. "I missed him, too. And as I got older, and you kept talking about law school…"

She looked up at her dad, surprised to see tears in his eyes. "You would look over my briefs in the evenings," he said raggedly. "I loved those hours, because that was when I missed Jack the most. And you had a knack for understanding. I probably pushed too hard…but, Molly, you don't have to leave. We can cut your hours. I know you've been working extra hard."

"You called me about cases while I was on my vacation," she chided gently. "I want off the merry-go-round, Dad. I'm tired of doling out the spoils of marriage and sorting out custody battles of people who act more like children than their own kids. I want to use my superpowers for good." She tried a smile. "You brought me up to be smart and independent, but I've made all my life decisions so far based on what would make you and Mom happy, and to somehow atone for what happened with Jack."

"Atone?" Olivia's perfectly plucked brow wrinkled. "What on earth would you have to atone for?"

She would not cry. She wouldn't. She looked up and said clearly, "He saved me, and then he died. Maybe it should have been me."

Charles went over and sat next to her, reaching for her hand. "God, no. What happened to him was an accident. Have you carried this around all this time? Sweetheart, you deserve to be happy and fulfilled. Don't you ever think differently. And if we somehow added to any pressure, I'm so sorry." He squeezed her fingers. "We love you... for you."

"Even if that means leaving the firm?"

"Even then, though I'll hate it." He smiled tenderly. "I'm sorry for being a grouchy old bear about you going away."

"It's not your fault, Dad. I just want to choose me for a while."

They all took a moment to wipe their noses and regain their composure. "Does that mean you're leaving law behind?" Olivia asked. "What will you do?"

Molly shook her head. "Not leaving it behind. The first thing I'm doing is helping out a new opioid center on the Cape. I learned about it at the charity event where I bid on the trip. It's a good cause and I can be of use there."

"And after that?"

"I don't know. I thought I had another project, but it turns out it's a conflict of interest. I'm going to take some time to figure things out." She looked at both of them. "This vacation was the first one I've ever taken on my own, and I'm nearly thirty. I went from high school to college to law school to work with no breaks. I want to take one now. Really have a look at my options and go from there."

"You're sure you can't do that while staying at the firm? We can reduce your caseload."

She met her dad's gaze and guilt slid through her. "Dad, I'm so sorry. I know this is hardest for you. And I love that you want me there and that you have so much faith in me. I feel like in order to follow my dreams, I'm crushing yours."

Silence dropped over them for a few moments, but then Charles straightened and put his hand over hers on the sofa. "You're not crushing mine. I wanted to raise a daughter who was smart and successful and strong. You're all of those things. I've been selfish for too long, Molly. You shouldn't stay because of me. That being said, there will always be an office for you. Always."

"Dad," she whispered, incredibly touched. "I thought you were going to be mad. You said on the phone you wanted me to come to my senses."

"And so I did. I would love nothing more than to have you work beside me, but I can't make that choice for you. It sounds as if you already made too many choices based on what you thought we wanted."

Olivia leaned forward. "Sweetie, we never wanted you to try to fill Jack's shoes. The only person you ever have to be is you."

Tears clogged Molly's throat as she tried not to cry—again. The most "her" she'd ever been was on that trip, and that was the woman Eric had fallen in love with. That was the woman who'd fallen in love with him. And she'd played right into his insecurities. She'd known that people saw the money first and not the man, and she'd done exactly the same thing by asking him to abandon a business deal just because she'd asked him to.

No wonder he'd been hurt. She'd taken their relationship and reduced it to dollars and cents and favors, all because she'd been all full of herself and her dreams.

Tears spilled over her lashes and she gave a big sniff, chagrined at crying during before-dinner drinks. This wasn't a delicate sniffle, but tears she couldn't control that just kept coming.

Charles got up and found some tissues somewhere and pressed them into her hand. "Don't cry, sweetie. It's fine now."

Olivia stood up and came to the sofa.

"Charles, you're a smart man, but this isn't about a job. This is a broken-heart sort of cry, so maybe you can check on dinner."

Molly laughed even as she was crying. Olivia didn't always speak up, but when she did it was with a dry, practical tone that bordered on sarcastic. Molly blew her nose in the tissues as Charles made a hasty exit and her mother sat down beside her.

"So you met someone on the trip."

She nodded. "And I blew it. I mean, it was going to be hard anyway, but…yeah."

"Oh, I doubt you blew it all by yourself. Just about everything takes two. You should know that in your line of work."

It was true. There was the odd case where clearly one partner was entirely innocent in the breakdown of a marriage, but more often it was failures on both sides. She'd been blaming herself, but Eric hadn't even given her a chance. She remembered what he'd said…something about leaving being hard but their fight making it a lot easier.

Maybe she'd been foolish, but he'd been a coward.

"It's okay. It wouldn't have worked out anyway. He's based out of Montreal and I'm here."

"Here and unemployed. Still, you knew

each other a week and a half, right? And there would be immigration things to work out. Big step for a relationship that young."

"Yeah."

"What's he like?"

For a moment, the words *unreachable* and *stubborn* came to mind, but then she remembered their long talks and the way he held her in his arms when he slept, tucked in against his body, as if afraid she'd somehow slip away.

"He's successful and confident on the outside, and gentle and funny on the inside," she murmured, dabbing her eyes with the tissues. "His dad abandoned them when he was a little boy, so he and his brothers grew up looking after their mom. He used to help her through panic attacks, and worked to help with the family finances."

"And what does he do now?"

"He's got his own company and a bazillion dollars."

Olivia snorted. "Good Lord. We told you to aim high, but wow."

"That's the problem." The worst of the tears were over now, and she straightened a bit and gave another sniff. "I asked him for a favor because he has the money and power to grant it."

"And he gets asked that all the time and thought you were different?"

Molly nodded. "How'd you know?"

Olivia put her arm around Molly's shoulders. "You know my mom and dad are old money. Your dad was working his way through law school. I was used to boys wanting to date me because I was the right kind of girl to take home to their mamas. I studied English and history and dressed the right way and my daddy had connections. Your dad didn't know who I was and didn't give a damn if I had money or not. I married him. Against your grandparents' wishes, by the way. I didn't bring any of the money with me, but I didn't care."

"I never knew that about you guys."

She shrugged. "We fell in love. That was just it."

Molly sighed, the ache inside her growing. "I think I did, too, Mom. He's amazing and handsome and wonderful and smart. Until I blew it."

"So try to fix it."

"He wouldn't talk to me before I left."

"So? Good Lord, child. You are the most persistent, stubborn woman I know. Since when do you give up when faced with *no*?"

Her mom was right. She hadn't even fought for him. "I don't know where to start."

"You could try calling or emailing. Open the channels of dialogue."

It was true. He still had all the pictures and video of their trip. It was a way in, perhaps. "Look at you," Molly said, smiling a little. "Relationship counselor while Dad handles the breakups."

"We balance each other out. Now listen. Stay and have dinner and get your bearings again. Then think about touching base. If you really care about him, reach out. If it's the end, it's the end. But at least you will have tried."

Molly leaned over and hugged her mom. "I love you, you know that?"

"I know. And we love you, too. Your father will get over your leaving, too. You just go be happy."

She would. If it was the last thing she did.

Eric pulled into the drive in front of a small bungalow in Laval. Three other cars sat in the driveway; his made the fourth and filled the remaining paved space. It was Sunday and they were all here, just as he knew they'd be. Maman had always made a big

deal about Sunday dinners and being together as a family.

He hadn't been to one in years.

Taking a huge breath, he got out of his car,
walked to the front door and, feeling incredibly awkward, pushed the doorbell.

His mother answered, her dark hair showing streaks of gray, her eyes with crinkles at
the corners and laugh lines at the edges of
her lips. She'd aged, but she looked happy.
And her face blanked when she saw him.

"*Mon Dieu!* Eric. *Vraiment?*"

"*Oui*, Maman." He offered a small smile.
"May I come in?"

"Of course! The boys are here. And all
the kids."

"*Je sais. C'est dimanche.*" He laughed.
"Tell me it's roast beef and mashed potatoes…"

Her eyes lightened. "Welcome home," she
said simply and opened the door wider.

The house was bustling with children a
variety of ages, slamming in and out of the
door that led to the backyard. His sisters-
in-law were all in the kitchen, helping with
the meal, the "boys" sitting at the table with
beers, talking. An odd silence fell over the
group when he stepped across the threshold.

Adam, the youngest, cursed under his

breath in surprise. And Robert—Bobby—lifted his eyebrows. "Eric. This is unexpected."

"I know. I should have called, but I was afraid you'd all tell me not to come."

The silence let him know that he wasn't being afforded a hero's welcome. Not that he deserved it, but this was no prodigal-son moment.

Janette, Adam's wife, twisted the top off a beer and handed it over with a small smile. He took it, gratefully, just to have something in his hands.

"Something is on your mind, *oui*?" Robert asked and used his foot to nudge out a chair.

"It is. I need to apologize. When Papa left us, I felt this huge responsibility to make sure we were okay as a family."

"You did a great job," his mother said, patting his arm as she deposited a stack of plates on the table. "You took on so much, at such a young age."

"But I made mistakes. I was so focused on providing us with material…well, not even comforts. Necessities. I started to equate my role as provider with one of love. And as a result, I alienated all of you. I just want to say I'm sorry. You're my family first."

Adam looked up. "When we started the dealership, you weren't exactly supportive of our abilities. You offered us cash. Like we couldn't do it on our own."

"I know." He finally sat in the chair and let out a sigh. "Look, those early years after he left, they were really tough. You guys were small and maybe you don't remember, but I promised myself that no one in my family would ever have to be in that position ever again. So my misguided way of showing I cared for you was also arrogant and self-serving. I can't change the past, but I want to be a part of this family again. If there's a place for me."

He looked up and saw his mother's eyes brimming with tears. Robert cleared his throat, got up and slapped Eric on the shoulder. "Then you should have brought the beer," he said, just before a broad smile spread across his face. He ruffled Eric's hair before reaching for his wife, who was also smiling. "It's about time."

His mother nodded. "I thank you for this house, and for all you've given us. But we really just wanted you."

It reminded him so much of something Molly would say that his heart gave a lurch.

And as the family dinner was served, he realized this was a pretty good place to make a change.

Two days later, Eric tapped his fingers on his keyboard without actually pressing the keys. The email had come through this morning and he still hadn't answered it. He didn't know how. Truth was, he didn't like how he'd behaved on that last day. She'd wanted to talk and he'd shut her down and walked away. Now, with a few weeks' distance, he could put that last morning in perspective. Had she been wrong to ask him? Probably. But had her motives been calculated? He highly doubted it. Everything he knew about her—in his head and in his heart—said that she wasn't the kind to take advantage of him over money.

She'd been caught up in the idea and hadn't thought things through. And boy, had he punished her for that. All because he was a coward and it had given him the out he hadn't realized he was looking for.

The words *unlovable* and *emotionally unavailable* came back to bite him, too, thanks to Murielle's parting shots. The only good thing to happen since his trip was the visit to see his family. A bridge had been tentatively built. They were family, and that counted for more than anything.

Which brought him back to the email on his screen. From Molly. She'd left the family firm after all and was taking time to evaluate her options. Meanwhile, she was wondering if she could have some of the pictures from the trip after they'd smashed their phones. And then she'd ended the email with "Best wishes, Molly."

So very polite. When all he could think about was their time together. He'd meant what he said at Butchart Gardens. He had been falling for her...was already over half in love with her. It had scared him to death and what happened that last morning had given him the excuse he needed to run.

Because it wasn't just her he hadn't trusted. It was himself. And love in general. Time away from her hadn't changed his feelings one bit.

He told his assistant to hold his calls for a half hour and instead went through the pictures and videos he'd downloaded to the cloud. There were several of scenery and wildlife, but also many featuring her...on the river, in her kayak, laughing around the campfire. One at the museum and even in a few group pictures. The last few days they'd taken a couple of selfies; one in particular he liked in the double kayak, with his face up front and her behind him, looking like a goofy kind of photobomb. And another in Butchart Gardens, of her on the carousel, whimsically happy.

The chances of them working out were slim, but he couldn't stay angry at her forever, not when he'd acted—reacted—the way he had.

So he shared the folder with her and told her she could have any of the photos and videos she wanted from the trip. That he hoped she was doing well.

Once that was done, he turned his attention back to work. Now Molly was on his mind, though, so he made a call to a colleague in Boston and asked about her. If she were working to mount some sort of challenge to his acquisition of Atlantic Bionics, he wanted to know about it.

Ten minutes later he hung up with a strange feeling in his chest.

She wasn't on the project at all.

An email notification popped up on his screen and he clicked on it. It was a reply from Molly.

Thanks. I really wanted to have some photos to commemorate the trip. I do hope things are going well for you, Eric. And want you to know that I did leave my practice and that I did not take on the Atlantic Bionics thing. It would have been a conflict of interest, and you were right. It was wrong of me to have asked that of you.

He swallowed roughly and then typed back a response.

I shouldn't have reacted as I did, either. I was too harsh. I know I have my reasons but that doesn't excuse my behavior. I'm glad we're not leaving things as we did that morning in Victoria.

Then he hesitated, wondering if he dare get more personal. Before he could change his mind, he added two sentences.

I hope you're on your way to being happier. You deserve it.

Then he signed his name and hit Send.

He didn't receive a reply until the next day, when her name popped up in his inbox when he opened his email after lunch. His heart did this little flutter thing just from seeing her name there, and his finger hovered over the mouse button, wanting to open it, wondering if he should.

Nothing had really changed. He was still in Montreal and she was in Boston. Even if they were both committed to try a relationship, it would be incredibly difficult. And clearly, after his reaction in the seaplane that day, he was far from being ready for a commitment. He had a lot of trust issues to work through, going back many years.

But it was Molly, and he couldn't just delete it without reading. He could read it and not reply, right?

He clicked on her name and brought up the message.

Hi Eric,

I went through all the pictures and the video and, wow! You got some great shots. Thank you for sharing them. And for everything, even helping me smash my phone. It helped to talk to my parents when I got home, and we're all okay with me going in a new direction. Surprisingly so. I hope you've had a chance to see your family. I know you were thinking of doing that.

I also want to say... I'm sorry. Sorry for ruining things on that last day when really the whole time with you was pretty magical. Even

the first day when you walked in on my bath.
You showed me that I had a sense of adventure just waiting to come out, and that I could
let go and fall for someone. I know we didn't
work out, but those were both incredible gifts
that I'll always be grateful for.

Thanks for replying and giving me a chance
to say how I feel. I hated leaving things with
anger and hurt.

Love, Molly

She was thanking him. Him! For giving
her gifts that she'd had all along anyway. He
should be the one thanking her. He'd never
met a purer soul than Molly, and a hard ball
of loneliness settled in the pit of his stomach. He missed her. God, he even woke in
the morning hoping to feel her in the sheets
beside him and she wasn't there. He wanted
to see her bright smile, or her flashing eyes,
when she got irritated.

He scrolled through his other messages,
trying to put the thought of her to the back of
his mind. They were close to closing on the
Bionics deal, and once that was done, he'd…

He paused. Once they closed this deal,
he'd move on to the next deal, and the next.

Molly's words came back to him. "You're

like that guy in *Pretty Woman*. He didn't build or make anything, either."

She was right. He didn't. He bought and discarded just as quickly, making a profit as he went. He could justify it all he wanted, from a business perspective, but the truth was he had never seen anything all the way through. Not even his marriage. His priorities had been upside down for years.

Eric tapped his fingertips on his desk, wondering if he were being absolutely crazy. He pulled up some files, ran some numbers. Grabbed a coffee and played around some more, and then popped out to his assistant's office. "Hey, Greg? I need to call a meeting."

CHAPTER THIRTEEN

MOLLY WAITED OUTSIDE the Boylston Street café and tried not to hyperventilate. When Eric had messaged and asked her to meet for lunch during his business trip, she'd agreed. She wanted to see him. Needed to. Maybe this whole thing would be for naught when they were in the real world. It was entirely possible that their affair had been a vacation thing and, when put in the actual context of their lives, would prove to be a nonstarter.

Of course, there was also the chance that she would see him and want to throw herself into his arms because she'd missed him that much.

She figured he was in town about the deal and she wasn't going to ask him about it. Truthfully, it was none of her business. Just this morning she'd met with the executive director of a local nonprofit and she was hopeful that soon she'd be gainfully employed, after only three weeks at loose ends. It was far less glamorous than her previous position, and the pay was nowhere near close to the same, but it was a start, and she felt as if she might help make a difference in the lives of some underprivileged kids. At least it felt like a worthwhile purpose.

The September day was cool, so for her interview she'd dressed in black leggings with knee-high heeled boots, a tunic-style sweater in china blue and a scarf looped carelessly around her neck. While the outfit was slightly more casual than she'd normally wear, she'd dressed it up with her favorite Coach bag and several silver bangles.

She'd be lying if she said she hadn't dressed with Eric in mind, too.

She caught sight of him crossing the street and her heart thudded against her ribs. Oh, he looked so good. He was in a suit, the button of his jacket undone, but wearing a tie, and he looked delicious. Their eyes met and there was the initial shock of recognition, and then a smile bloomed on his face, a glorious expression of welcome and happiness. She grinned back and walked toward him, trying to keep her steps measured and calm. When they met in the middle of the sidewalk, there was an awkward moment. She wanted nothing more than to lean in and greet him with a kiss. It felt like the natural thing to do. But there was too much undecided and unsaid, so instead she moved in for a hug.

It seemed he had the same idea because his gaze dropped to her mouth, but then he put his arms around her briefly before stepping back and cradling her face in his hands.

"Damn, but it's good to see you."

She couldn't stop smiling. "You, too."

He dropped his hands and let out a breath. "I was nervous as hell about that. I wasn't sure you'd want to see me."

"I know." She looked up at him and shrugged, the memory of their last morning together washing over her. "The way we left things…"

"I'm so sorry about that."

"Me too."

"I've got a lot to tell you. Should we go in?"

The café had, in Molly's opinion, the best sandwiches in Boston, and that was saying something. She was famished—between the interview and meeting Eric she hadn't been able to eat a thing all day. They were seated fairly quickly and the drink orders were taken before they had a chance to talk at all. Once their sparkling water arrived, they each took a sip and then met each other's eyes.

"You look good, Molly."

"So do you. No yoga pants for me today."

"How's the break treating you? You getting some perspective?"

She toyed with her glass. "Actually, I had an interview today. For a nonprofit here in the city. I'll know in the next few days if it's a go."

"Nothing high-profile anymore?" He took another sip and put down his glass.

"No, at least not now. If we're being honest… I'm pretty set financially, between what I made at the firm and, well, my trust fund. Ugh. That makes me sound like such a spoiled brat. Anyway, the pay cut won't affect me much. And the hours are decent. I'm still donating my time to the opioid clinic."

"You sound happier."

"I am. This new job… The foundation works with underprivileged kids to help them with postsecondary education." She went on to tell him about some of the initiatives they had in place and the scholarship programs. "Applying felt right," she said, opening her menu. "When I was doing family law, the custody battles were what used to get me the most. It was always the kids. Maybe now I can help put lives together rather than pulling them apart."

He nodded. "You like children."

"I haven't been around them a whole lot. Being an only child, I have no nieces or nephews. My friends are just getting married or starting families now. But I met families in my job, and the kids always looked so lost or angry."

"Which is why I'm glad Murielle and I didn't have children. I didn't make time for her, you know? So I wouldn't have with kids, either. But I like them. My brothers' kids are all in school. One just turned thirteen. He's really fun. Into video games and all charm, too. If he goes into the dealership, he'll be a top salesman, no question."

She laughed a little. It was hard to believe she was actually sitting across from him after over a month apart. "You saw your family, then?"

He nodded. "I did. It's been good. More than good."

The waitress came over and took their orders, and they handed over their menus before resuming their conversation.

"Molly, I came here today to tell you that you were right."

Her lips dropped open in surprise. "Me? Right? How?"

"About my business. About me. It didn't quite click until I went back home and took a good hard look at my family, my relationships, my business."

"I don't quite follow."

He put his hands on the edge of the table. "As much as I hate to admit it, I'm a runner. Remember what you said to me when I told you what business I was in? You told me that I break things up into parts and sell them. I don't fix them or rebuild them—the only thing I've built is EPC Industries, and really, that's just the mechanism I use to make money and do business with short-term commitments."

"I remember." She wasn't sure at all where he was going with it, but she was ready to listen. Clearly this was a big thing to him.

"It wasn't until I talked to my mom that I started to understand and put it all together. I was young when my dad left us. My mom told me she remembers me asking if it was my fault. That if I'd been a better son, my dad would have stayed with us. Of course it wasn't my fault. I know that now. But at the time, I suppose it made sense that I closed myself off a bit. My mom was devastated. So was I. And if I never allowed myself to get too invested in anything, I'd never be hurt like that again."

It was a huge revelation to be dropped in the middle of a café, and Molly was prevented from replying by the arrival of their meals. The sandwiches came with fresh-cut house fries, and Molly dipped one in ketchup before biting off the end. It gave her a little more time to consider her response, because right now she was picturing Eric as a hurt little boy, curled up in his mother's arms. It gave her heart a painful twist to think of him that lost and insecure.

"You know," she finally said, her voice soft, "I used to see kids like you in my office. Sitting with their moms or dads, wondering what the hell had happened to their secure world. Have you spoken to your father since he left?"

"He sent a letter when each of us graduated. I burned it."

She nodded. No contact, no child support—Eric's mom had been truly on her own. "Your mother must be a very strong woman. Three boys would have been a challenge."

"She's the best."

"Which is why it hurt when your relationship got strained."

He nodded again. "My ego. And my over-developed sense of self-preservation. I'm very good at making money. It doesn't seem like a noble endeavor, but I think it stems from the fact that we never had enough growing up. We barely made rent. Sometimes we turned the heat off to save money. My grandparents gave us food a lot."

"So you went a little Scarlett O'Hara? I'll never be hungry again?"

"Yeah. Except I think I went overboard with that ambition and somehow equated that with being, I don't know, better. My brothers are great men. Family men, running a business and supporting them." He gave her a soft smile. "I'm starting to see that I can learn a lot from them."

"That's a huge deal. Maybe the trip away was good for you on a personal development level, too."

"I'm a work in progress, what can I say?" He grinned and picked up his sandwich.

She smiled a little. "Aren't we all? Thank you for telling me, Eric. I'm so glad you and your family are getting along better."

They each took a bite of their sandwiches, though for Molly it seemed more out of obligation than actual hunger at this point. So far he'd said nothing about *their* relationship.

Eric dabbed his lips and then put down his napkin. "There's more," he said. "About Atlantic Bionics."

She dipped another fry, trying to stay nonchalant but unbearably curious. "All right. What's up?"

"I had a meeting this morning. I'm still buying the company, but we're staying. I mean, we're not dismantling anything. I'm going to help them fix it. Whether that means expansion or moving the manufacturing arm somewhere else and ramping up R and D, I don't know. But you were right in the plane that morning. It's a good company with important work. So EPC is going to invest the time and resources to get it in the black again."

She nearly dropped her French fry. "Are you serious?"

"Completely." He smiled at her. "And can I tell you a little secret? It feels really good. I want to see this through. I have you to thank for that."

So that was his big bombshell for today. He was going all in with the Bionics deal. Apologizing for his reaction in the seaplane. A part of her rejoiced. This was the man who'd been on the trip. Seeing him so happy, so changed…was incredible.

But he hadn't said anything about them. Nothing about still caring for her or wanting to be with her. When they'd agreed to meet, she hadn't really known what to expect or what she really wanted. Now that she didn't have it, she knew what she'd wanted was to be asked for another chance. To give them a try and see if they could make it work.

He hadn't mentioned any of that. Just that it was good to see her. Thanking her for her "help."

Her mind darted back to the trip and the nights they'd spent together. It had been transcendent. Maybe the real world was different after all. That was the Eric she wanted back. But it didn't seem to be what he was offering, and it was hard not to feel disappointed.

"Are you okay? You've hardly touched your sandwich."

She looked down at the lobster roll and felt her appetite disappear. "Oh. It's fine. I think I'm just hitting post-interview letdown or something. I didn't sleep much last night."

Her lack of sleep had had nothing to do with the interview and everything to do with seeing him again.

"I'm sorry. I hope you get it, though. You deserve to be happy, Molly."

"I'm working my way there, I think." But her earlier enthusiasm was gone.

"That's good. Really good."

The conversation had got stilted, and they ate a respectable amount before Molly pushed back her plate and said she was full, leaving half her sandwich and two-thirds of her fries. "The portions are very big," she offered and took a drink of her water.

"I should get back, too. I'm staying in Waltham for a few days, working out of a temporary office on site."

She had nothing on her schedule. Absolutely nothing for the evening. Her empty apartment and a few hours of volunteer work the next day. At this rate she was thinking she'd need to get a cat because she was lonely.

He paid the bill and they walked outside into the September sunshine. It was Molly's favorite time of year, when the days cooled but the leaves hadn't really started to turn much yet. The sun seemed to gild everything with a mellow glow. It did a little to pick up her mood, but not much.

"It was really good to see you, Eric," she said, folding her hands in front of her. "I'm so glad you're finding your way to being happier."

"It's not perfect," he replied, his dark eyes holding hers. "There are a few pieces missing. But I'm working on it. I hope to have everything in place really soon."

"I'm sure you'll figure it out." She offered her warmest smile, while crying a bit on the inside. This wasn't the Eric she'd got to know in Canada. This Eric was more reserved. Cautious. Or perhaps, less interested.

"Can I call you again, Molly? I'm going to be in Massachusetts quite often as we get this off the ground."

"Of course." What else could she say?

"Okay. Take care, all right? And I'll be in touch."

He leaned forward and kissed the crest of her cheek. During the brief contact, she closed her eyes and held her breath, trying to imprint the moment on her memory forever. The feel of his soft lips, the nearness of him, the scent of his cologne. All too soon he stepped back. His eyes were questioning as he looked into her face, but he said nothing.

"Bye, Eric," she said quietly and turned away.

All it would have taken was one word, one small question, to ask if she still wanted to try. If she cared, or wanted to go on a date, or whatever. But he hadn't said anything. He'd made all these great and tough changes in his life. Surely he could have said how he felt.

But he'd said nothing, and that said it all.

She gathered her dignity and walked away.

He'd blown it.

Eric sat in his temporary office in Waltham and put his head into his hands. It had been going so well at lunch, and then he'd watched the shadow fall over her face and she'd completely closed off. Then he hadn't known what to do. The timing had been all wrong to open up about his feelings, and the more the lunch went on, the more he'd panicked about what to say. In the end he hadn't said half of what he'd wanted to, but what was the point if Molly wasn't interested?

He simply didn't understand. She'd looked so happy to see him, and then in the middle of lunch she'd just looked…disappointed. What had he done wrong?

There was a knock on the frame of his door and one of the office assistants poked her head inside. "Mr. Chambault? There's a Dr. O'Neill here to see you. He's a bit early for his appointment."

"That's okay. Send him in."

"Would you like some coffee, sir? I can bring some in."

"That would be great, Megan. Thank you."

She beamed, seemingly pleased by the simple fact that he'd remembered her name and been polite. Good heavens. What had their work environment been like before?

When Dr. O'Neill stepped inside Eric's office, Eric recognized him immediately. He'd wondered why the name sounded familiar—now he knew. He'd been Molly's date at the benefit. And the one to ask her to work with them to save the facility.

He shouldn't be jealous, but he was. This man and Molly were friends. Heck, maybe they were more than friends. But he was also one of the top vascular surgeons in the country. He cared a lot about the future of Atlantic Bionics and had a wealth of knowledge to share.

"Come in, Dr. O'Neill. Megan's coming back with some coffee. Is there anything else you'd like?"

They shook hands—a good firm handshake—and then O'Neill shook his head. "No, I'm fine. I got off shift a while ago and grabbed a bite at the hospital. I see you're settling in."

"I am. I head back to Montreal at the first

of the week, but I'm going to keep an office here, too, so I can be hands-on now and again. This is all new territory to me."

"So I gather. We were surprised to hear you were going to stick it out, to be honest."

"No more surprised than me," he admitted, gesturing toward a plush seating area. "But sometimes life throws us curveballs. Good ones."

"Like Molly Quinn?"

Eric stilled, but O'Neill took a seat in one of the chairs and crossed his ankle over his knee.

Eric followed suit, relaxing his face into an easy smile. He'd been in business too long to let his weaknesses show. "Of course. Molly's great. And she was right about this place."

"Eric… Can I call you Eric? And you can call me Ryan. I didn't come to see you about the business. Not today, anyway."

He raised an eyebrow. "Ryan, if this is about Molly… I'm not about to talk about my personal life. If you want to talk about the consultancy…"

Ryan waved a hand and wrinkled his brow, looking annoyed. "Yeah, yeah. You know I'll help with that. This place has potential that has never been fully realized. It needs your business acumen and my medical expertise. Or others like me. You might not want me after I say what I've come to say."

Megan picked that moment to interrupt with coffee. She put the tray down on the coffee table and quietly left. Both men picked up their cups and sipped, leaving their coffee black.

"Clearly you have an agenda, so you'd better say your piece."

"All right. Molly is a damn fine woman. She's tough when it comes to the courtroom and a marshmallow underneath. She's got ethics coming out of her ears and she truly cares about people."

"You sound as if you're half in love with her."

"And so I might have been, but she's not interested. Believe me, I've tried. We're friends, and that's all."

Eric's collar started to feel a bit tight.

"You've tried?" He looked into the surgeon's face. They were about the same age; O'Neill was maybe a few years older. His eyes were sharp and intelligent, with crinkles at the corners that made him look as if he was always holding back a joke. The thought of him making moves on Molly...

"Don't worry. She made it very clear she's not interested in me that way. First, I was her client. Then we became friends. Anytime I asked her out, she made it clear that we were just platonic. Two nights ago we went for drinks. I wanted to update her on this situation, but instead she gave me the whole lowdown on who you were to her. To say I was surprised to hear her talk about you at such length is an understatement."

Eric took a slow inhalation and kept his grip even on his coffee cup. "I'm surprised. We met for lunch the other day. It was pleasant, but that was all." God. Had she told Ryan everything about their trip, too? It didn't seem like Molly, but after lunch the other day, he'd realized that he really didn't know her as well as he thought he did.

"Pleasant." Ryan chuckled. "Eric, you've got your poker face on and that's fine, but if you care about her at all, you'll listen to what I have to say. Then if you can sit there and look me in the eye and say she doesn't matter, I'll let it drop and we can move on to talking about amputations, prosthetics and orthotics."

Eric said nothing, just gestured as if to say that Ryan had the floor.

Ryan put down his coffee. "I've known Molly for a while, and I can honestly say we're friends. I bug her about it now and again and we end up as each other's plus-one. I care about her a lot. I'm not denying that I'd be thrilled if she actually said yes. But I want her to be happy, and she was so unhappy the other night I know that she's carrying around a lot of feelings.

"She told me about your trip, and the kayaking and zip-lining and her panic attack and how amazing you were. It was clear to me that she'd fallen for you big-time. So when she explained what had happened that morning in Victoria, I felt horribly responsible. I didn't know who you were. She'd messaged me about leaving the firm and looking for some work she could sink her teeth into. I thought I was doing her a favor."

"You were," Eric admitted, trying to keep his emotions level. "She was really excited about doing something new."

"And then you stomped on it. Not that I blame you entirely, and neither does she. And I'm not going to get into a 'he said, she said' with you. What I know is that whatever happened over lunch the other day, she was hurt and disappointed."

Eric sat forward in his chair. "Listen, we were talking and then all of a sudden she clammed up and she shut down. What was I supposed to do?"

Ryan sighed. "Look, as men we can be pretty clueless when it comes to, well, clues. Here's what I know. Molly said you were talking about your family and the business and how great it all was…but you never said anything about her or your feelings for her. She thought you might be meeting her to try to start over. When she realized you weren't…"

Eric sat back in his chair and for once didn't worry about his poker face. That was what she thought? That he hadn't wanted to talk about them? He'd just been getting to it when she clammed up and then what was he supposed to say?

He closed his eyes for a second and sighed.

When he opened them again, Ryan was watching him with a slightly amused expression. "Oh, you don't need to look so pleased with yourself," he muttered grouchily. "I messed up again. And don't look so self-satisfied. Clearly neither of us is great when it comes to women. You were her client, after all."

Ryan chuckled. "Fair point, so I'll give it to you. Now I'm gonna ask you. Are you in love with her?"

He didn't even hesitate. "I'm in love with the woman I met on our trip. I think we're both wondering if that's who we are in real life."

"And how are you going to figure that out if you don't even try? Take her out on a date or something?"

"What are you now, a therapist?" Eric got up from his chair and paced to the window. "Look, I appreciate the advice. I do. But…" He stopped. But what? He was afraid? Hell, yes, he was afraid. But did he love her?

His biggest fear was that what they'd had wasn't real. The only way he could know for sure was to put himself out there. But that wasn't so easy to do. Not for a guy who had kept himself closed off for years.

"I'm just going by what she said and what she saw. She's miserable, Chambault. I think she went there hoping for a big reunion and she got everything but. How would you feel if she talked about how great her life was now but never mentioned that she wanted you to have a part in it?"

When put that way, it made sense. Perfect sense. And explained why he'd blown it so badly.

"I really messed it up, huh?" he said quietly, turning back to face the other man.

"Yeah, you did. Hey, we'll figure out this company thing. I'm incredibly happy that you're sticking around and I'm on board with working with you. But I really came here today because of Molly. I kind of feel responsible for what happened, and I want her to be happy. Even if it's not with me."

Eric looked straight into Ryan's face. He was dead serious. He truly cared about Molly if he was willing to step aside if it meant she'd be happy. That Ryan seemed to think it might be with him…well, he'd never been one to give up easily. Not when it was something he really wanted.

And the truth was, he wanted Molly in his life. Wanted it more than he wanted to protect himself and his heart. It had taken until now for him to truly realize it.

"It needs to be perfect," he said, shoving his hand in his pocket and gripping his coffee cup.

A grin spread across Ryan's face. "Then I have an idea. What you need to do is…"

CHAPTER FOURTEEN

IT HAD BEEN a surprise to get Ryan's invitation to dinner at the Merchant Seafarer, but Molly had agreed for several reasons. One, the hotel marked the moment in time when she'd embarked on a life change, and despite her heartbreak, she didn't actually regret any of it. Two, the Seafarer had some of the best cuisine in New England, and a gorgeous view of the Atlantic from the verandas. And three, it was her birthday, and it felt as if everyone had forgotten. Dinner with a friend on your birthday beat out staying home with a pint of ice cream and the leftover half of a bottle of wine every time.

He'd sent a car for her, to drive her all the way from Boston to Nantucket. When she'd protested, he'd said it was a birthday present and to be quiet, in his humorous kind of way. So she'd thanked him, and when the car had arrived this afternoon, she'd slipped into the back seat and decided to enjoy the ride. She put in earbuds and listened to her favorite playlist for a while, then simply sat and enjoyed the scenery, even nodding off once for fifteen minutes or so. When she woke, she opened her compact and tidied her makeup. He'd told her to dress up, so she'd donned a dress that had been in her closet for ages but she'd never worn: a knee-length black cocktail dress that skimmed over every curve to her waist and then flared out in a fifties-style skirt. It was very Rosemary Clooney–esque, and made Molly feel as if she were embracing her figure rather than fighting it.

And absolutely no Spanx. Those ten pounds were fine right where they were.

The car pulled up to the pillared portico at the resort and Molly tucked her earbuds into her clutch along with her phone—the new one she'd bought to replace the cheap pay-as-you-go she'd bought in Victoria. An attendant opened her door, and she stepped out, feeling rather princess-like. It was only the realization that she was meeting Ryan that put a damper on the fairy-tale feeling. He was nice enough. He was a good friend. But he'd never be anything more.

And then she looked up at the steps and her heart stopped.

It wasn't Ryan standing there. It was Eric, dressed in a flawless tuxedo, watching her with bald admiration in his eyes.

She took one step, then another. He waited, let her ascend the steps on her own, and when she was two steps away, he held out his hand.

It was trembling.

She put her hand in his, palm to palm, and his fingers closed around hers.

"You're not Ryan," she murmured, looking into his eyes.

"No. It was part of the surprise. Is it okay that it's me?"

She considered saying no, of not putting herself out there to be hurt again, but when all was said and done, she and Eric had always spoken the truth. "It's more than okay," she admitted, her voice shaking. "I just don't understand."

"You will," he assured her. "I promise." He lifted their joined hands and kissed her fingers. "Tonight I'm going to say all the things I should have said earlier. And then, Molly, you're going to have my heart in your hands."

She wanted to press him to ask what that meant, but she'd already learned that with Eric, anticipation was exciting and oh, so worth it. She did have one request, though, that she couldn't wait for. "Could you do me one thing, before we go in?" she asked.

"What's that?"

She lifted her chin. "Could you kiss me, please?"

His eyes locked with hers, suddenly hot and intense. *"Oui, ma chère,"* he answered, taking the one step necessary to be close enough. His lashes settled on his cheeks as he closed his eyes and his lips touched hers. The kiss was gentle, yet deliberate and persuasive. When they both opened their eyes, she was sure there were probably stars in hers and her knees were wobbly.

Nothing had changed. Not for her. And he was here, right now, in a designer tux, holding her hand, taking her for dinner in one of the most exclusive resorts in New England.

That had to be worth something.

So she let him lead her inside to a private corner of the dining room, where they indulged in oysters and duck and wine and a pumpkin-spice soufflé that was so incredible Molly almost wished she had room for more. By tacit agreement, they talked about day-to-day events during the meal, but always Molly was aware of the way he looked at her and somehow got the feeling that the things they really needed to say would be said before the night was over. Indeed, as they lingered over Irish coffee, Eric reached over and took her hand. "Molly, there were things I should have said the other day at lunch that I didn't. I'd like to say them now. Will you come outside with me?"

She nodded, feeling that familiar and welcome fluttering in her belly at his words. This was the Eric she remembered. Subtly seductive, so attentive. The man she'd dined with in Campbell River and in Tofino, when promises of the night to come were never spoken but always communicated.

Together they left the dining room and went outside to the enormous wraparound veranda that looked out over the vast Atlantic. The sun was setting now, and a chill had settled on the air. Eric took one look at her bare shoulders and removed his jacket, draping it over hers. "I forgot how cool it gets in the evening," he said.

"It's okay. I love being out here and smelling the sea air. Hearing the waves. It reminds me of our base camp."

"It was an amazing trip." He twined his fingers with hers as they approached the white railing. "In so many ways, but mostly because you were there. Always challenging me."

She shook her head and exhaled out of her nose, a little scoff at his last words. "Me? I was the one so afraid half the time."

"But even then, you were challenging me to open up. I couldn't help myself, Molly. That's what's so miraculous about it all."

He turned to her and held both her hands. "When we had lunch together, I told you all about my family and the business decision, but I didn't tell you the most important part. I thought you didn't want to hear it. Fortunately a friend of yours set me straight."

"Ryan."

He nodded. "He came to me and told me I was being an idiot for letting you go and not fighting for you. When I looked past my jealousy, I knew he was right."

"He set this up for you tonight."

"I wasn't sure you'd come if I asked. And I wanted it to be special." He squeezed her fingers. "He's a good guy, your friend Ryan." He emphasized the word *friend*, making her laugh a little.

"So what did Ryan say?"

Eric held her gaze as he said, "That I should tell you that none of this would have happened without you. That you taught me how to open my heart. If I hadn't done that, I couldn't have tried again with my family. I wouldn't have decided on this business decision. And I wouldn't be able to stand here and tell you without a doubt that I fell in love with you on that trip and I'd like the chance to be in love with you now, if you feel the same way."

"You love me?"

He nodded. "I was afraid that the trip was a fantasy. Like, maybe not who we really were. But, Molly, I really think that for those ten days we were exactly who we are deep down, without the daily grind dragging us down and shaping us into... I don't know. There was a freedom to it and I love who that Molly is. I love the way she makes me laugh, and smile, and think about things, and pushes me to relax, and makes me want to be a better man with a better heart."

"Oh, Eric..."

"You make me want to live better, Molly. The money doesn't provide security. Only love does that, and I've been denying it for too long. But I need you to make the picture complete."

Tears gathered on her lashes and she blinked quickly to clear them away. She didn't want him to be blurry or wobbly when she looked into his eyes and said the words she'd wanted to when she'd seen him again.

"Since I came home, every time I took a step forward I wanted to call you and share it with you. When we started emailing, I thought perhaps we'd moved past what happened that last morning. I never wanted us to be over, Eric. Not that day on the plane, not at lunch. I always wanted us to at least try. I know it was a vacation, but I've never felt this way about anyone before."

"I was such an idiot that day." He took her hand and placed it on his heart, over the crisp white material of his shirt. "You wanted to talk and we could have worked it out. The truth was I got such cold feet. I felt so much for you it terrified me, and I used it as an excuse to run. Molly, I was married and I can honestly say that I've never felt this way before. Like if you walk away you'll be taking my heart with you. I've kept my heart locked up for so long, afraid of having it broken. But you—you got past all those barriers. I don't know how, but you did."

"You were left when you were so little, by the person who was supposed to love you the most," she said softly, putting her other hand on his cheek. "That little boy is still afraid of being hurt. And the man he's become is so compelling, so strong and tender. Maybe you didn't want to open yourself up to those emotions, but the way you took care of me the night I had my nightmare…" Her lips trembled as emotion swept over her. "The nights we made love. I can't just forget those times. They're a part of me now."

"And of me." He pulled her closer and wrapped his arms around her, tuxedo jacket and all. "I want to try, Molly. I don't know how we're going to work out the long-distance thing, though having business in the state helps a lot. But I'm committed, and that's something new for me. I'm committed because I love you, and I can't imagine my life without you. Please say you're willing to try."

This was what she'd wanted all along. Not a guarantee that everything would work out perfectly; all her years as a family-law attorney had thoroughly disabused her of that idea. But she wanted someone who loved her enough to try, to attempt to move mountains because she was worth it. Someone who accepted her for who she was, with no adjustments necessary. Not a trophy. Not a stand-in for her brother. Just her. And she was enough.

"Of course I'm willing to try. That trip?

It was a once-in-a-lifetime trip. It just follows that falling in love is a once-in-a-lifetime event, too. I'd be foolish to let that slip through my fingers."

His fingers were now twining through her hair, and she loved the feel of them against her scalp, playing with the strands as his gaze delved deeply into hers. "Yes," he agreed, "you would."

And then he kissed her properly, with the sound of the breakers on the sand behind them and the salt tang of the sea in the air. She lifted her arms and his jacket fell to the veranda floor, but she didn't care. She curled into his embrace and kissed him back, finally feeling as if she were truly home. Where she belonged.

"I love you, Eric," she whispered, tightening her arms around his neck. "I wasn't looking for it, didn't expect it, but I love you."

"I love you, too," he whispered, hugging her so tightly she could barely take a good breath.

He kissed her again, then let go and held her hand. "So where do we go from here?" he asked.

She grinned. "That's easy. It doesn't matter, as long as we go together. For now, you'll be close by with the new company, and it's a short, direct flight to Montreal. We'll start there and figure everything else out as we go."

"Sounds perfect." He pulled her in against his side, and they watched the waves together. "Molly, that night of the benefit? I lost the bid, but right now I'm feeling like I just won the jackpot."

EPILOGUE

CHRISTMAS HAD BEEN spent in Montreal with his family, going to midnight mass, eating *tourtière* and wrapping presents for Eric's nieces and nephews. Molly had never had a Christmas like it in her life, and seeing Eric laughing with his brothers warmed her heart. His family had been welcoming, the sisters-in-law teasing her good-naturedly about her poor French, and welcoming her into the fold as if they'd known her for years. She'd never had siblings, so it was an overwhelming but lovely experience.

Now it was New Year's Eve, and they were spending it in Boston, with Molly's parents. There'd be a New Year's Day brunch, but for right now, they were at First Night, stomping their feet to stay warm, enjoying live music at Boston Common and, in a few moments, the fireworks after the countdown.

It had been a year for change, and the year

ahead was looking even brighter. Most of all, for Molly, was the fact that she was fulfilled in a way she'd never been before. She had no regrets about her career change, and she was so deeply in love that some days she thought she might burst with it.

Eric looked down at her as the crowd started counting from ten. He held her hands in his and bestowed her with a gaze so full of love she nearly melted with it. How had she got so lucky?

When the cheers of "Happy New Year!" rose in the air, he wrapped his arms around her, thick coats and all, and kissed her soundly on the mouth. His lips and the tip of his nose were cold, but his mouth was not, and she opened herself up to the kiss, caring little about the fact that they were in public.

The first boom sounded: the fireworks had started.

But instead of turning toward them, Eric reached into his pocket and withdrew a small box. And when she met his gaze, she saw nerves there, and fear. Dear God, did he really think she could say no? And yet this was a man who'd thought for many years that his worth was based on his balance sheet, and his insecurity reached in and touched her right in the heart.

He opened the jeweler's box, where an enormous diamond winked up at her.

"Molly? Will you marry me?"

She took off her gloves and shoved them into her coat pocket. "Just try to stop me," she replied and held out her hand. "Put it on me, Eric, and make it official. Because I love you more than words can say."

He chuckled, an emotional sound as the sky exploded around them, then took the ring from the box and slid it over her knuckle, folding her hand and tucking it inside his palm. "Don't ever change, Moll," he murmured, kissing her knuckles. "I want you to keep telling me how it is for at least fifty years."

"At least," she agreed, and then with a huge smile, they turned to watch the rest of the fireworks as they ushered in a brand-new year.

* * * * *